Catherine Cookson was born in East Jarrow and the place of her birth provides the background she so vividly creates in many of her novels. Although acclaimed as a regional writer – her novel THE ROUND TOWER won the Winifred Holtby Award for the best regional novel of 1968 – her readership spreads throughout the world. Her work has been translated into twelve languages and Corgi alone has 40,000,000 copies of her novels in print, including those written under the name of Catherine Marchant.

Mrs Cookson was born the illegitimate daughter of a poverty-stricken woman, Kate, whom she believed to be her older sister. Catherine began work in service but eventually moved south to Hastings where she met and married a local grammar school master. At the age of forty she began writing with great success about the lives of the working-class people of the North-East with whom she had grown up, including her intriguing autobiography, OUR KATE. Her many bestselling novels have established her as one of the most popular of contemporary women novelists.

Mrs Cookson now lives in Northumberland.

Other books by Catherine Cookson published by Corgi

THE SLOW AWAKENING
THE GAMBLING MAN
THE GIRL
THE MAN WHO CRIED
THE CINDER PATH
THE WHIP
HAMILTON
THE BLACK VELVET GOWN
GOODBYE HAMILTON
A DINNER OF HERBS
HAROLD
THE MOTH
THE PARSON'S DAUGHTER
THE CULTURED HANDMAIDEN
THE HARROGATE SECRET

The Mallen Trilogy
THE MALLEN STREAK
THE MALLEN GIRL
THE MALLEN LITTER

The Tilly Trotter Trilogy
TILLY TROTTER
TILLY TROTTER WED
TILLY TROTTER WIDOWED

The Bill Bailey Trilogy
BILL BAILEY
BILL BAILEY'S LOT
BILL BAILEY'S DAUGHTER

Autobiography
CATHERINE COOKSON COUNTRY

Catherine Cookson

The Iron Façade

CORGI BOOKS

THE IRON FAÇADE
A CORGI BOOK 0 552 10780 8

Originally published in Great Britain by
William Heinemann Ltd.

PRINTING HISTORY
Heinemann edition published 1976
Corgi edition published 1978
Corgi edition reprinted 1978 (twice)
Corgi edition reprinted 1979
Corgi edition reissued 1980
Corgi edition reprinted 1981
Corgi edition reprinted 1983
Corgi edition reprinted 1984
Corgi edition reprinted 1985
Corgi edition reprinted 1986
Corgi edition reissued 1990
Corgi Canada edition published 1991

This book is set in 10/12pt Joanna
by Chippendale Type, Otley, West Yorkshire.

Corgi Books are published by Transworld Publishers Ltd., 61–63 Uxbridge Road, Ealing, London W5 5SA, in Australia by Transworld Publishers (Australia) Pty. Ltd., 15–23 Helles Avenue, Moorebank, NSW 2170, and in New Zealand by Transworld Publishers (N.Z.) Ltd., Cnr. Moselle and Waipareira Avenues, Henderson, Auckland.

Printed and bound in Canada.

The Iron Façade

CHAPTER ONE

'I'm going to be sick again.'

'Oh, Aunt Maggie!'

'I – I can't help it. I – don't like it any better than you— Stop the car!'

'I didn't mean it like that. Hang on, I must find a place to park off the road.'

When I saw my aunt put her hand swiftly to her mouth, I didn't wait to find a suitable place on the grass verge but pulled the car abruptly to a stop and, getting out, ran round the bonnet and was only in time to hold her head as she retched for a second time into the ditch.

Straightening up and wiping her mouth, she muttered weakly, 'I'm sorry.'

'Oh, Aunt Maggie, there's nothing to be sorry for. Come on.' I turned her about and led her towards the car again.

'There is to me. I'm supposed to be looking after you.'

'It'll do me good to think of somebody else for a time.'

'It might at that, but I don't want to be sick to give you that opportunity.' Although she was leaning weakly against a fender, my aunt glanced at me with a shadow of the twinkle that was nearly always present in her eyes. She then said, 'If only I had a drink of soda water I'd be all right. Unless I've lost my bearings altogether, there's a village somewhere near here. We've crossed the River Eden, passed Appleby, Colby and Strickland. Now before we get to Brampton, there's this little place I remember called Borne Coote.'

'You should have let us stop in Appleby and have a meal as I suggested.'

My aunt turned her eyes to mine again, then lowered her head and leaned heavily against the side of the car. I turned and walked a few steps along the grass verge and looked down over rolling green hills, down, down, down to a valley, where the faint froth of water was discernible. Beyond, the hills rose again to fall, I knew, on the other side to more burns and rivulets and cascading water. This was Cumberland, a county new to me, and although beautiful in some of the areas through which I had come, it was wild and desolate in others. But that was how I wanted it – desolate – lonely. That was why I had suggested that we stop for a meal in Appleby. Aunt Maggie, thoughtful as ever, had said she wasn't hungry; all she wanted was to reach our destination.

We had started from Eastbourne shortly after five o'clock that morning. Just before we left, after she had been round the house to give a last check-up to windows and doors, Aunt stopped for a moment in the hall and touching me gently on the cheek had said, 'You'll sleep tonight, Pru, without pills, I promise you.' Then, with her ability to bring laughter out of nothing she exclaimed, 'Pru, pills and promise. You wouldn't like to partake of a little repast before we depart would you?' If laughter had not been dead in me, I would have laughed. I only smiled at her and we had left.

'It's a grand sight, isn't it?'

I hadn't been aware that she had joined me. I turned to her. 'Are you feeling better?'

'Yes, yes,' she nodded. Then she added: 'Until the next time. So much for palliative pills.'

'It's this heat,' I said. 'It's so unexpected.'

Aunt Maggie was gently shaking the neck of her blouse back and forth as she answered. 'It must be ninety – and at the end of August. There's one good thing about it – it won't last. I can't stand the heat, not this kind at any rate. But look, isn't it bonny?'

My aunt moved her hand in a wide half-circle, and my eyes followed its course and saw that the scene was indeed bonny. It should stir me as lovely scenery had always stirred me; my breath should be catching with the effect of all this rolling beauty; my heart should be singing with the knowledge that I was to live in it for three months; but there was no emotional response in me, nothing but an icy numbness which melted only to make room for fear – fear that made me walk with my head down and my eyes fixed on the ground.

'Remember,' Aunt Maggie had chided me, 'when you used to be afraid of getting a double chin? – Come on, lift that head up.'

Could I be the same person who had once had a horror of a double chin, the person who had been careful to sit upright in a chair and never to cross her legs in case her hips spread? It had been said, and not so very long before, that Prudence Dudley, besides being clever, had a lovely figure, and a remarkable face – not beautiful, but remarkable. Yet there was someone who had said that the face went beyond beauty. He had said that there was plainness and prettiness, then beauty, and, after beauty, exquisiteness. That exquisiteness had nothing to do with beauty or prettiness, it was something on its own – yes, that had once been said to me . . .

'Now stop it, you're tired. Come along, stop it.'

My Aunt Maggie's hands were covering mine, pulling them from the lapels of my suit, easing the fingers away one after the other. Her voice, stern now, was saying, 'Pru, you're tired. That's all. Stop contemplating. Remember, you've had bad patches before – they come and they pass. Remember that – they pass.'

I was in the car now sitting at the wheel. My body had stopped trembling, but the perspiration was running down my face, and it was only faintly that I heard my voice saying, 'I'd better take a couple of pills.'

'But there's no water.'

'I'll swallow them dry.'

'No. No, don't do that, my dear. I seem to remember this road. Go along there and turn off left. I'm almost certain you'll come to Borne Coote. There'll be a café, or some such place in it. Perhaps we'll each get a drink. If not soda water, a cup of tea.'

My hands began to shake again as I started the car but I kept repeating Aunt Maggie's formula, 'It will pass.'

A few minutes later, there was the road Aunt had

remembered, and a half mile further along it, we ran into the village and saw immediately, and to my consternation, that there was something on. Most of the villages we had passed through had been sleepy, almost deserted, places. Whether this was natural to them or due to the unexpected heat, I didn't know. But now, at a quarter to two in the afternoon during the hottest part of the day, the village was abuzz. There were at least a dozen cars, none of them very smart, lined up along one side of a low granite block wall which bordered a cemetery as bright with flowers as any park. And sitting among the flowers, on the grass and gravestones, were groups of people, all laughing, joyous people. Similar groups were repeated at intervals all along the main street.

Neither of us spoke. My Aunt Maggie didn't make the comment that would have been natural, 'It's a wedding.' But, when we had reached the end of the street and had come to a little square with a stone cross in its centre, she said, 'Over there, look, where it says "Ices", we'll get a drink of some sort.'

The shop, I saw at once, sold everything, including paraffin oil, but there was no one in it. Aunt Maggie knocked on the counter, and when she did so for the third time, she accompanied it with a sharp command: 'Hello, there!' Receiving no answer to her call, she did not, even now, make the obvious statement, 'I bet they've gone to the wedding,' but, taking a basketful of groceries from off an upturned lemonade box, she placed it on the floor, then sat down on the box and, pointing to what looked like a butter cask, said, 'Sit yourself down on that and we'll wait. It's cool in here, anyway.'

I didn't want to sit down; I wanted to stand, or

rather walk. At this moment I wanted to walk quickly away from everything, especially from this village and all its laughing people. I knew the signs, I knew what this feeling would lead to. My heart would begin to jerk, then race. Then my limbs would tremble, and this would be followed by that dreadful feeling that I was about to die. But wasn't that what I wanted – to die? Yes, but not in that fear-ridden way. They – they being the doctors – said I could conquer the feeling. They all said it was up to me now . . .

'Well, Aa never! Aa never knew there was anybody in. It's the weddin' you know. Aa was out back lookin' over the top wall. You can see the side path into the church from there. Well, now.'

The little thin wisp of a woman with the painfully straight hair and bright bead eyes looked from one to the other of us. Then, her gaze settling on me, she said in rapid sympathetic tones, 'It's a drink you'd be wantin'. I should say you do. You look as white as a strip of lint. It's this heat. Did you ever know anythin' like it? And us steppin' into September. Just like the weather, isn't it – contrary? But could you have it better for a weddin'?'

'Do you happen to have any soda water?'

'Soda water?' The little woman confronted Aunt Maggie. 'That's a thing we haven't got. Practically everything on God's earth we've got in this place – ' she spread out her short arms ' – but no soda water. "Syphons," I said. That's what I said to Talbot. "We want syphons." "Who's going to pay four bob or more for a syphon?" Talbot asked. But, as I said, "That's only at the beginning, you'd get them refilled for next to nothing." But he wouldn't hear of it. No, we haven't got any soda water, but the next best thing's ice-cream soda – look!' She pointed to a row of coloured bottles. 'How about that?'

'Yes, I'll try that – anything.' Aunt Maggie was moving her head slowly in assent.

'And you, miss?' The bead eyes were turned on me now. 'Are you going to share, or would you like one to yourself?'

'Is it possible to have a cup of tea?'

'Oh–h!' As if the eyes were being moved by a switch, they now did a series of jerks between my aunt and myself. And with this action, the little woman made it evident that tea was going to be a bit of a bother at this moment, so I put in quickly, 'Oh, it's all right; I'll have a bottle of lemonade.'

'Well, now, not that Aa wouldn't make it for you, an', if Talbot had been in, Aa would have done it like a shot. Aa would do it if you'd hang on, but oh, Aa'd like to see the weddin' and Aa daren't leave the shop, you see, not for long like. But, if you like, Aa could put the kettle on and come back in a few minutes.'

'It's all right, I'll just have the lemonade.'

'You sure now?' She bent towards me as if trying to persuade me out of my choice.

At this point, the shop door opened abruptly to the sound of heavy breathing and the sight of a hand thrust in towards where Aunt Maggie was sitting on the lemonade box brought our eyes towards the round, red, slightly indignant face of the newcomer.

'Oh, it's on the floor at t'other side.' The little woman darted forward, picked up the basket and pushed it into the outstretched hand. 'The lady wanted to sit down . . . Is she coming yet?'

There were a couple of wheezy breaths before the woman answered, 'No, not due for five minutes yet. I've run all the way.'

The basket and the round face disappeared, and the little woman, addressing Aunt Maggie, said, 'That's Alice Merely. She used to work up at McVeighs' for years, and her mother and father afore her. The weddin's for McVeighs', but it's not one of the McVeighs. Miss Doris is a Slater. Her and little Janie were old McVeigh's young sister's children, if you see what I mean. They've lived with the McVeighs since their mother died. It's Miss Doris who's being married this day.' The little woman suddenly stopped and patting her lips with a child-like gesture at her forgetfulness exclaimed, 'Oh! You want glasses.'

As she dived into the back room, Aunt Maggie signalled to me with raised eyebrows.

'There you are. Mind, it's fizzy, and it might go all over your frock . . . You're not from hereabouts?' The shopwoman was holding the bottle over the glass as she put the question.

'No. No, I'm not.'

'Aa thought you weren't. But Aa thought you might be.' She was now looking over her shoulder with a cunning expression on her face towards Aunt Maggie. 'Somethin' in your voice, like ours sort of.'

'Well, it should be,' said Aunt Maggie. 'I was born not so far from here – in Evenwood near Bishop Auckland.'

'Well, Aa never! Do you know the McVeighs then? Have you come for the weddin'?'

The froth was spilling onto the shirt of my grey

wool suit, and gently I guided the woman's hand aside and took the glass from her.

'No. No, I don't know the McVeighs. Bishop Auckland isn't exactly on the doorstep,' my aunt informed her.

'No, it isn't that, I grant you, an' I'm well aware of it.' The little figure was inclined to bristle now. 'But the McVeighs are known far and wide. If you ever lived in the county, you couldn't help but hear of the mad McVeighs. Of course, it was the old man an' his father before him that made the name. The two that are left now aren't very hectic, although Mr Davie is mad enough in his own way. Yet everybody in the county knows the McVeighs.'

'It must be more than thirty years since I was in these parts, you must forgive me.' There was a small note of sarcasm in my aunt's voice. It was a danger signal that brought me from my low seat to my feet. My lovable kind aunt had a tongue like a rapier at times. Although we owed nothing in courtesy to this woman, for she had not put herself out very much on our account, I still did not want her to be hurt. I did not want anybody to be hurt. Some part of me was always wishing for a miracle that would make mankind immune to hurts and the results thereof.

'How much do I owe you?'

'Well, you're not taking the bottles.' The eyes were darting now between the two bottles. 'That'll be elevenpence each. You haven't drunk half of it but that's not my fault, is it? One and tenpence, please.'

We were just going out of the door when the little woman, almost on my heels, addressed me pointedly, practically turning her back on Aunt Maggie as she asked, 'Are you stayin' hereabouts or are you just passin' through?'

As my mouth opened to answer, Aunt Maggie's sharp voice came over her shoulder, 'We're just passing through.'

While I started the car once again, Aunt Maggie, looking straight ahead and speaking under her breath, exclaimed, 'Nosy Parker! These out-of-the-way villages seem to breed them.'

'I should have asked the way.'

'Yes, I suppose you should. She'd have known every step of the road, I bet. Look, there's a car drawing up in front. It looks like some form of taxi. I'll ask him.'

I drew our car once more to a halt, and Aunt Maggie, leaning out of the window and looking along the kerb to where a man was alighting from a dignified pre-war Bentley, called, 'Can you please tell us the way to Lowtherbeck at Roger's Cross?'

The man came to the car and bent down towards my aunt. He was tall, thin, with a grey moustache and a solemn face, the only solemn face I had seen in the whole village. His voice sounded serious as he asked, 'Are you for the weddin'?'

Although I could only see the back of my Aunt Maggie's head, I knew that she had closed her eyes. Her voice told me so.

'We are not going to the wedding,' she answered him. 'We would just like to know the way to Lowtherbeck, if you don't mind.'

'No – I – don't – mind.' The man's voice was slow and held the same note of controlled patience as did Aunt Maggie's. I could remember the time when I would have laughed at the implication in their tones. 'Go round the stone cross there and out of the village that way until you come to the three roads. If you want to get there quickly, take the gully sharp left. It's steep and it's narrow, but it will bring you to the very door and it will save you a couple of miles or more. But if you want to do it in leisurely fashion, take the middle road. There's no shelter from the sun that way, you'll be dead on top of the fells, but it's a good road and five miles long to the very inch – now, is there anything more I can do for you?'

My Aunt Maggie drew her head back inside the car. Her eyes were turned sideways up at him. 'No, thank you,' she said. 'You have been very explicit.'

'The – pleasure – is – mine – madam.'

Oh, if only I hadn't forgotten the way to laugh! I set the car moving slowly forward, and, as we rounded the cross, I glanced to the right. The tall man was standing beside the little woman storekeeper outside the shop watching our departure.

'That,' said Aunt Maggie slowing, 'is Talbot, I bet me bottom dollar.' And then she burst out laughing.

'Oh, Aunt Maggie,' I said.

'Oh, lass,' she said, mimicking my tone. Then she added, 'Oh, well, we know where we're bound for, five miles to the inch or down the narrow gully straight to the front door. Which is it to be? I leave it to you.'

I took the narrow gully.

And you could almost say it *was* a gully. It was a track between two high banks beyond which towered tall trees, a great part of their trunks covered by an undergrowth, the whole making a deep shade over the roadway which was most welcome after the glare of the sun.

'Ah, this is nice.'

As Aunt Maggie spoke, I turned the wheel sharply to follow a bend in the lane, the bend was followed by another and yet another very much on the hairpin style. My foot was already on the brake as the road itself was steep, but, on turning the third bend, I instinctively pressed it down hard, for there, tearing up the incline towards me at a pace that should never have been attempted on such a gradient, was a big black car. My mind registered it as an old Rover.

My hand brake was tight on, and, although I had shut off my engine, I still held my foot on the brake as I stared from my elevated position down through two windscreens into a large face that was screwed up in a sort of amazed perplexity – and something else.

The cars were almost bonnet to bonnet. I did not move from my position at the wheel. Only with my eyes did I follow the other driver's movements. He wrenched his car door open; he took the few steps which brought him to my open window; now his face was thrust through it at me.

His appearance was strange, to say the least. At first I thought I had been looking down at an old man, a white-haired old man – this man could not have been more than thirty-five – his hair was so fair as to look almost bleached. This was emphasized by the colour of his skin which had that ruddy brownness produced by sun, rain and wind. But it was much later in the day before I realized I had taken any note of his appearance, for at this moment he was awakening in me a feeling that had been dormant for many months. It was anger.

'What the hell are you doing on this road?'

My answer was so trite that, again, it was only later when going over the incident in my mind that I censured myself for it; it was the kind of double cliché that I was careful to keep out of my own writing, and criticized when I found it in the writing of others.

'Who do you think you're talking to?' I demanded. 'It's a free country. At least, so I understood.'

Under the chemical reaction of the man's anger, the irises in his dark blue eyes were widening, and he held his breath before bringing out, with a slowness that was in itself a calculated insult, 'Would you care to take a look into that car?' He thrust his arm out. 'You will notice, unless your eyesight is as much affected as your road sense, that there's a bride sitting in it. And, naturally, she's on her way to her wedding – at least, she was . . . What is more, she happens to be late already.'

I did not do as he commanded and look at the bride. I hadn't noticed there was a bride in the car although I had taken in a silvery mass behind the dark blur of the driver. I was about to say, 'Well, you'll just have to go back because I cannot reverse up this steep hill,' when Aunt Maggie spoke my thoughts and in a much cooler manner than I could have achieved. Yet there was a cutting edge in her voice. Bending across me, she peered up at his supercilious face as she said, 'If you're in such a hurry, I shouldn't stand there wasting time. You back down the hill until we can pass you, because we cannot reverse backwards round these bends.'

Again the man held his breath, but not for so long this time, and his tone when he answered was rapid, 'Madam, there are two more cars at this moment setting away from the bottom of the bank, if they are not already halfway up it.'

'Well then!' Aunt Maggie laid particular stress on these two words with which she usually preceded any admonitory sentence. 'Well then! They'll have to back, too, and the quicker you get started the more likelihood you have of getting to the church, if not on time, then sometime today.'

'Davie.'

The man turned his head sharply towards a hand which was waving out of the car window. Evidently the bride was not going to risk damaging her head-dress by getting out. I was looking at her now through the intervening windscreens and an awful feeling of resentment flooded my body. The longer I could keep her waiting, the better I would like it.

'No, no! Don't be like that.' The voice was loud in my head. I looked at the man and said, 'I can't attempt this winding road in reverse; it's too rough. How far before I can pass you downhill?'

I wasn't looking at the man's eyes but at his mouth – it was very thin for such a large face. It was a cruel mouth, I thought. All men were cruel – I hated men, all of them – all of them – all of them! My mind was beginning to race again. 'It's not true.' The voice in my mind was speaking again. 'You only hate one.'

'No – two,' I almost answered the inner voice vocally because, at this moment, I was hating this big face, and these dark blue eyes, and this head covered with odd bleached fair hair.

My gaze, lifting to the man's now, was undoubtedly expressing my feelings and, as his eyes held mine, I shouldn't have been surprised if his hand had come up and struck me. But almost in one leap, he was back at the wheel of his car and talking rapidly to the girl behind him. I could not hear what he was saying for the noise of the engine – doubtless, the substance was vitriolic.

With a driving dexterity that deserved credit, he backed the big car down the incline, and, as I followed, Aunt Maggie's voice came to me, cautiously saying, 'Now, go steady. Don't be silly, go steady.'

Did she know that I had a strong desire to drive my bonnet forward and crash that arrogant bully off the road?

For a moment, the black car disappeared round yet another bend and when it came into view again it had stopped. From my superior position I saw, at two points of the road lower down, two more stationary cars. The man was out of the Rover now and running down towards them. The sound of his voice shouting orders came to me, but now I wasn't paying much attention to it – I was looking once again through the windscreens straight at the bride, who was looking at me. She was leaning forward over the front seat staring at us.

I willed my Aunt Maggie not to say, 'My! she's bonny. Isn't it a pity – all this mix-up?'

I gave another extra tug to the hand brake before I started to get out of the car.

Now Aunt Maggie put her hand on my arm and her voice had an underlying note of anxiety as she said, 'Now, Pru.' Then, again, as I shook off her hold and stepped into the road, she repeated, louder this time, 'Now, Pru!'

I walked the few steps to the window of the Rover, and there was the girl's face staring at me. I have no idea what I first intended to say, nor what impulse brought me to this action, but I surprised myself I know when I did speak.

'I'm sorry for all this,' I said.

'Oh, don't worry.' The happy smile on the girl's face pained me. The kindness in her words pained me. I would have felt much better if, like the man, she had raged. The bride-to-be spoke now as if I knew all about her. 'Jimmy'll wait for years. Don't worry. Anyway, it isn't your fault, no matter how Davie goes on. I've always said there should be a notice at the top of the lane.'

'This way was recommended to us.'

'It was?' There was surprise in the girl's voice. 'Who told you that?'

'A man in the village.'

'Now I wonder who that could have been?'

I found that I was amazed at the girl's attitude. She was going to her wedding and her pleasant pretty face was twisted slightly with enquiry as she wondered who my informant had been. All her concern at this moment seemed to be taken up with this wondering.

From the corner of my eye, I saw the man running back up the bank, and, after saying once again, 'I'm sorry,' I retreated hastily towards my car. But before

I was settled in the seat, the face was hanging over me again, the voice snapping out orders.

'About half a mile down the bank there's a grass verge – sort of. It's on a slope. See what you can do about it.'

The Rover was moving backwards again, but more slowly now for the driver had adjusted its speed to that of the cars behind. It seemed a long time before we came to the grass verge. Even then I wouldn't have recognized it as such but for the gesticulating of the man at the wheel in front.

Aunt Maggie objected, 'You can't get on there; that's a bank.'

I stopped the car. Yes, it was a bank – not much of a bank as banks go, but nevertheless a bank. My car was a modern one and had little weight. Likely the old Rover in front of me could have taken this slope and held it, but I could see myself doing a back somersault into the road again.

My head was out of the car and I was shouting, 'It's too steep.'

Now the big face was facing me at an angle. 'You can take it. Look, stay where you are a minute an' I'll show you.'

I watched the Rover mount the bank and hang there at a dangerous angle.

'You'll never be able to do that. Don't you attempt it,' Aunt Maggie protested.

'I'm not going to let that big head get the better of me.' I answered Aunt Maggie without looking at her. Then, as the Rover backed once again onto the road, I went into first gear and slowly, very slowly, mounted the incline.

'Oh, my God, we'll be over! I tell you we'll be over!'

'Be quiet, Aunt Maggie.'

To my surprise, Aunt Maggie was silent. When she grabbed at the handle to balance herself, for she was now leaning heavily against the car, I said tersely, 'Don't move.'

Her answer, a deep intake of breath, was smothered under the noise of the cars as, one after the other with throttles open, they sped past us. The other two cars were packed to capacity and I was aware of a number of bobbing heads and eyes turned in our direction. Then they were gone and we were alone.

For the first time I realized that the road was no longer shaded with trees but was open to the glare of the sun. Gently I reversed and cautiously edged the car back down the bank onto the road once more.

'Thank God!'

Although Aunt Maggie uses the expression 'Thank God!' a number of times a day, it is not in an irreverent way. Not at all. When you hear my aunt use the words 'Thank God', you know they mean just exactly that, and, at this moment, I was endorsing them.

'You did that very well, lass. I would have said nobody could have stuck on that slope without overturning. Well, that was an experience. They say that all experience is grist for the mill, but I can do without that kind, what do you say?'

'I would like to tell that big lout what I think of him!'

*

I had been thinking along those lines, but with no intention of voicing my thoughts. But that was the way of things. Although I had no conscious wish to hurt anyone either by word or deed, I seemed to have little control in mastering my emotions. That was one of the reasons I wanted to get away from people. I knew as yet I wasn't ready for civilized society, in which you do not say immediately what you think, in which your thoughts, before they leave the channels of your mind, must be sorted out lest they embarrass or hurt the hearer. No, I knew I wasn't ready for an ordered civilized community, for when I spoke I wanted to speak nothing but the truth, plain fact and truth – and life can be very uncomfortable with unadorned fact and truth.

This phase, the doctors had told me, was a natural reaction to having suffered due to lies. All my life I had suffered the one way or another because of lies. I had been brought up on lies. I can still hear my mother saying to me, 'Tell Daddy I've gone over to Kay's.' I was eight before I knew that Kay was a man. I was twelve when I knew that Father did not go to the continent for business alone but for pleasure as well, a special kind of pleasure. And yet for years they had both lived together, been polite to each other, talked to each other, and acted as if nothing unusual were happening.

I cannot believe now that I was just fourteen when the farce of the three of us living as if we were a normal family ended, for I seemed to have been playing at their game for a great number of years. I say when the 'farce ended', for it ended only to break up into two separate farces, shameful and humiliating farces, at least to me. But not to my mother, or my father either.

My mother said, 'You will love it, darling; Joey is such fun. He's young and gay and has such a lovely boat. Oh, you will love it.'

I didn't love it, and I hated Joey.

When I had attended boarding school afterwards, I had spent half the holidays with each parent and I could never decide which I hated most, Joey's hands searching my waist or my father's bachelor apartment, which could be in France, Spain, or Italy – or wherever the fancy took him. Each apartment was presided over by a different housekeeper who did no work; but all of the housekeepers had one thing in common – they all had big busts – and they all disliked me as much as I did them.

I was seventeen when my mother divorced Joey and said that I must leave school and come and live with her – we 'had only each other'. Those were her words and I believed her. I didn't mind giving up the idea of going to university. I had only been working half-heartedly for it anyway. I knew what I wanted to be, I wanted to be a writer, and I couldn't see that I was going to be helped very much more by another three to four years of mental slogging.

Mother and I 'had only each other' for six weeks – then Ralph came on the scene. Ralph was four years younger than Mother, which made him thirty-one. Quite suddenly I was packed off to my father.

I was put in the first-class Pullman with chocolates, magazines, a travelling rug – like an old lady, and a last-minute present was thrust into my hand – it was a three-strand pearl necklace. Then Mummy was waving frantically from the platform, with Ralph by her side. Her eyes were full of tears – I swear she had a glycerine phial in her handkerchief. And so she was rid of me once again.

But that was one journey I did not complete. I got off at the next station, put my new yellow hide cases in the 'Left Luggage' office, and went to the coach station. A little over an hour later, I was sitting in the kitchen of my Aunt Maggie's house in Eastbourne. Her arms were around me and her tears, real tears, were mingling with mine as she pressed me to her, murmuring over and over again, 'Don't worry, my love. There now, there now. You'll stay with me. Just let them try to get you – just let them.'

They did try, but not overhard. My mother descended on the little house and accused her elder half-sister of being an interfering, frustrated old maid.

Was I coming back home?

No, I was not.

She would write to my father – something would be done about it.

Nothing was done about it. That was the humiliating thing. The knowledge that they were glad to be rid of me was more devastating than the game of tug-of-war they had played with me for years. And all the love and kindness Aunt Maggie showered on me couldn't make up for the feeling of being rejected, of being thrown aside, put out of the way.

I was eighteen when I first took ill, and neither of them came to see me. My father was in Australia by then. He sent me money to buy an expensive present and said he had been in touch with the doctor and I must get out and enjoy myself. My mother was in France on an extended honeymoon.

She, too, had been in touch with the doctor and her advice was similar to my father's. I must get out and enjoy myself. When she returned she would get Ralph to introduce me to some nice boys. With my looks I could pick and choose. But, in the meantime, I must get about and amuse myself. There was no better cure for – *nerves*!

Neither the doctor nor Aunt Maggie had called my illness 'nerves'. The doctor had said it was a form of exhaustion. I was so weak. I couldn't lift hand or foot. I lay in bed day after day looking out the window at the trees across the road through which I could glimpse the chimneys of the big empty house beyond. It was thinking about this house that brought vitality back into my body. I found I was filling the empty rooms with people and making up stories about them.

I made up several stories about the house and, always, the occupants were a close-knit family, a happy family. Then, one day, my dreams turned into reality. A family came to live in the house. It seemed to me at the time that I had conjured them up out of fantasy. It was a happy family; I became connected with it and the connection ruined my life.

It says somewhere in the Bible: 'And their second state was worse than their first.' This was true for me, too . . .

'Well I never!' These words must have escaped Aunt Maggie's guarded lips, for her lips were always guarded on any subject that might bring me added hurt.

The man in the village had said the road would

take us to the very door. And that is what it had done. The path had widened out into a kind of drive, and the drive encircled a large round of lawn, and, beyond it, stood the house – a replica of the house I had been thinking about only a moment ago. There were the steps leading to the front door, four in this case, the other house had six. And, on each side of the steps, there were two large bow windows. Above them were six long windows which spanned the front of the house. The windows in the other house had been footed with iron balconies. There were no balconies here, but the side of the house was almost covered along its ground-floor level and halfway up its height with a conservatory, an exact replica of that other conservatory.

'Well, we're here.' Aunt Maggie's voice was low. 'We'd better make ourselves known. Everything seems very quiet – no!'

It was at this point we turned and looked at each other, the same thought speaking from our eyes. We were at the bottom of a valley. It seemed a dead end and there was no other house to be seen. The wedding party must have come from here.

My Aunt Maggie was biting her lip and she pulled on it hard before saying, 'But this can't be Lowtherbeck! That woman said the name was McVeigh – I mean those concerned with the wedding.'

'No, "Slater", I think. She said the name was "Slater".'

'Well, Slater or McVeigh, that's got nothing to do with Cleverly, has it? Miss Flora Cleverly, that's the name on the letter.' Aunt Maggie rapidly opened her bag and, producing the last letter of the correspondence that had passed between her and the owner of the cottage we had taken, she tapped the signature, saying, 'Flora Cleverly!'

'Well, there's bound to be someone about. We'd better enquire – we can't just keep going on.'

Simultaneously we got out of the car and together we walked up the steps to the front door. It was wide open, showing a half-panelled hall with stairs leading off at the end. On a polished table to the left side of the door stood two twisted candlesticks with a bowl of roses between. The hall floor was bare except for one rug in its centre, and, although the boards showed the dusty marks of many feet, I could see from the surroundings it had been highly polished. I have always had an observant eye, seeming to take in everything at a glance. I suppose it is a natural part of a writer's stock in trade, and, from the first glimpse of the interior of this house, I sensed that there was little money about – at least not enough to keep up with the ordinary wear and tear of such an establishment – for, although I could only see two steps of the stairs, I noted that the stair carpet was worn, so worn it was torn in the middle of the treads.

After I had rung the bell for the third time, Aunt Maggie said, 'Let's walk around.'

So we went down the steps again and along the front of the house, but before we reached the second bow window we had both stopped again, our glances drawn to a length of whiteness stretching from the window to the other side of the room – a table laden with the wedding feast.

My Aunt Maggie's crisp tones brought my gaze

from the window. 'Well, I just can't understand this. There's only one thing I know: this can't be the place we're looking for.'

We were now on the side of the house opposite to the conservatory. This side was open to a courtyard – but an unusual type of courtyard, for it was bordered on one side with a hill of stark solid rock. On our journey over the fells, we had passed great outcrops of rock – the fells themselves were composed of such, as were sections of the hills and mountains – but it seemed odd to find the rock so near to the house when all around there was evidence of a green valley which was wooded in parts. The rock looked out of place, as if the house had been there first.

'Hello, there!' Aunt Maggie was calling now, her voice loud. 'Hello, there!' When there was no answer, she turned towards me and lifted her shoulders significantly. 'Surely there must be someone about – they couldn't leave the place to God and good neighbours and all the doors open and everything.'

My aunt was moving now towards the middle of the rock wall in which, oddly enough, there was a door – and the door stood open. I had turned and was looking towards the side of the house, which I realized was the kitchen side.

Aunt Maggie said, 'Here, a minute!'

Her tone was urgent, and when I walked towards the rock I thought how odd it was to see an ordinary doorway in that massive stone. The doorway spoke of a hollowness inside which belied the impression of the rock itself. Then I was standing by Aunt Maggie's side and she was pointing into the dim depths. As I peered I saw what had caused her exclamation.

'They grow mushrooms – look at the boxes. That must be a cave in there. But the smell! Still, it's fascinating.'

'Yes, yes, but let's try to find someone.' I wasn't interested in the mushrooms or the cave. Of a sudden, I was feeling very tired, physically tired; I had been at the wheel of the car for hours. What was more, I hadn't had a solid meal since six o'clock last night.

As we turned away, I almost tripped over a piece of wood at the foot of a small lean-to which covered an old rusty coke stove. I kicked it aside and said to Aunt Maggie, as she was going to some pains to close the door, 'I wouldn't shut it; it was likely left open for a purpose.'

I was to remember these words of mine some time later.

'This is fantastic,' said Aunt Maggie, dusting her hands. 'If this is Lowtherbeck, where are the Cleverlys in all this? Evidently, the bride is from here, and if she is, then so are those McVeighs.'

'Well, if that's the case—'

'Ssh! Look there.'

Stemming my rising indignation, I turned in the direction of Aunt Maggie's gaze. Standing at the corner of the house watching us from underneath lowered lids, I saw a young girl. The sun was full in my eyes and, from that distance, I guessed she could have been any age from fourteen to eighteen.

'Hello!' called Aunt Maggie. She moved forward and I followed her, and now we were standing close to the girl.

As I looked at this being, I felt a tremor pass through me. It wasn't a tremor of revulsion, but a feeling that always prepared me inwardly when I was confronted with something odd in nature. I have experienced it on a bus occasionally, and on board ships when sitting next to someone who looked quite ordinary, but proved to be slightly deranged.

However, it did not require any gift of insight or deep probing to know that standing before us was an unusual person. I was more puzzled than ever now about her age, but what intrigued me more was the beauty of the creature – immediately on looking at this girl, I had termed her in my mind a 'creature', a delicate, rather unearthly, creature. Her head was still inclined forward, but her eyes were wide open now and it was for all the world as if we were looking into the eyes of a young antelope. Her skin was cream-coloured – one could almost imagine that it would feel pleasantly warm to one's touch. Her mouth was full and beautifully shaped. But it was not the face that gave the impression of strangeness so much as the girl's body, for it seemed to droop; rather, it was relaxed like that of a very young child.

'Hello, my dear.' Aunt Maggie's voice was soft and low as if speaking to a child whom she did not want to startle. 'I think we are lost. We are looking for a house called Lowtherbeck at Roger's Cross. Can you help us?'

For answer, the girl turned slowly and pointed towards the house, and, as she did so, there slipped from her hand a book. As it fell to the ground, I saw that it was a Beatrix Potter book. There was nothing strange in that – this was Beatrix Potter's country – yet, was there not something extraordinary in a girl of this age reading such a baby book? Well, why not? I was still reading, at intervals, A. A. Milne's *Winnie-the-Pooh*. But there was a difference here, for this book seemed to be part of the girl. As if she were reclaiming part of herself, she stooped quickly, grabbed up the book, and held it to her chest with both hands.

'This is Lowtherbeck then?'

The lips parted, the head nodded and she said, 'Yes.' Her voice would indicate her age as six or seven years old.

Speaking for the first time and, also, keeping my voice low I asked, 'Does anyone called Cleverly live here?'

The head bowed again. 'Yes.'

Her answer surprised me. If the Cleverlys lived here, what were the McVeighs and Slaters doing in the same house? – all living together, apparently. If that were the case, that settled that. I was certainly not going to live within sight or speaking distance of the gentleman with the odd-coloured hair – cottage, or no cottage. We would have to find someplace else, even taking into account that already we had paid quite a substantial amount to reserve the place.

'My name is Fuller, and this is my niece Miss Dudley. We have rented a cottage near here, it belongs to—'

'The cottage – yes.'

The girl was smiling quite brightly now and nodding her head. Then, with a darting movement she ran past us onto the drive to the car and, opening the back door, she turned and glanced towards us before getting in.

Neither of us had moved, but Aunt Maggie exclaimed, 'Well, I never!'

With no more words, we went forward and took our places in the front seat.

Because of the luggage stacked on the back seat, the girl was sitting forward on the edge of it, and Aunt Maggie's face was close to the girl's as she asked, 'Will you show us the way?'

'Yes – round the side.'

'Which side, my dear?'

'Side of the house, 'course.' She laughed – the sound was slightly eerie.

'You'd better try it.' Aunt Maggie spoke under her breath.

I set the car in motion and edged it slowly down the path by the side of the house. It was just wide enough for us to pass. Then we came to what should have been the back of the house, but had more the appearance of a front façade because it was bordered by a wide terrace, which was now studded with deck-chairs and odd tables. Two French windows leading into the house were wide open.

I spoke over my shoulder, asking, 'Are you sure this is the way?'

'Yes.'

We passed the terrace, then a rose shrubbery and a vegetable garden.

'You're all right. There's been cars along here before.' Aunt Maggie pointed through the window. Then, turning round again, she asked of the girl, 'How far away is it?'

'By the Lil Water.'

The 'Lil' I knew to mean 'Little'.

Aunt Maggie's rejoinder was not, 'That doesn't help much,' as it might have been to anyone else – she only smiled at the girl and nodded her head before she turned towards the front again.

'Oh, look at that! Isn't it beautiful?'

The path had come abruptly into the open – it actually ran on the rim of a hill and the scene below was, indeed, beautiful. There again was the sparkle of water – not a rivulet this time, but a lake.

Aunt Maggie had twisted to the back seat once more. 'Is that the water?' She was pointing behind my back.

'No, that's the Big Water.'

'Oh!' Aunt Maggie, looking ahead, was muttering now. 'Little Water; Big Water, sounds as if we had struck an American Indian reservation.'

I was driving very carefully for there were only a couple of feet between the edge of the road and the steep sloping hillside.

'I wouldn't like to come along here on a dark night,' Aunt Maggie commented.

I endorsed this mentally and was beginning to censure myself for bringing the car along the path. We should have walked to the cottage first, yet it seemed as if it were a goodish way from the house or the girl wouldn't have got into the car. The path now took a deep curve and began to descend steeply. Leaving the sunlight, the trail entered the coolness of a small copse, but only for a few minutes; then we were in the sunlight again and I pulled the car slowly to a halt.

I knew, as I stared at the scene before me, that if nature alone could cure a troubled mind that I would soon be better. There to the right of us lay a small lake, bordered on one side by the continuation of the copse we had just passed through. On the opposite side, rose a hill covered with great patches of heather. Slowly I brought my gaze from the right and looked to the left.

Aunt Maggie was also looking in this direction. She turned her wonder-filled eyes towards me and breathed, 'My, isn't it bonny!'

'Bonny' was not the correct word to describe the cottage. It was two-storied and built of blocks of granite which in the late afternoon light, had a warm pink hue. Profuse clematis covered one corner and lent an added beauty to the stone. Before the door and the two windows were wide flagstones intersected with heather. There was nothing between the flagstones and the grass bank that sloped very gently towards the lake. A railing, a garden ornament, even a chair would have marred the whole at this moment. The lake and the cottage were one and I was to live here for three months.

For the moment I had forgotten about the man with the odd-coloured hair.

'Well, well!' Aunt Maggie was slowly moving towards the cottage now with the girl walking slightly in front of her, her face half turned towards my aunt as if she were leading her. And Aunt Maggie might have been speaking to herself, for I was still in the driving seat, but I caught her words as she said: 'She didn't exaggerate – "a haven of peace" she called it.'

And yes, that's what the letter had said, 'a haven of peace'. And the writer had added, 'I'm sure your niece will benefit from her stay, it's worked little miracles with a number of convalescents.' Recalling these words, I felt a quick stab of resentment, resentment that anyone should have lived in this cottage, should have come here before me. I was aware that the feeling was ridiculous and unreasonable.

I got out of the car and watched my aunt and the girl walk out of the sunlight into the dark shadow of the doorway, but I made no haste to follow them for I was experiencing another odd feeling. I was resenting the fact that Aunt Maggie was with me. I had the strangest desire that I should be alone in this place, along with the cottage and the lake. I turned my eyes to the water. A strip of it, near the right bank where the trees were, lay in shadow. The rest of the water was a magnet for the sun, and, as if being caressed with jewelled rain, the surface sparkled and shimmered. So bright was the reflection that I closed my eyes against its brilliance.

'Pru!'

I turned towards the cottage. There was Aunt Maggie beckoning me from the window. I walked slowly towards the door; when I reached the threshold I stopped. Nothing that I saw surprised me; I seemed to know exactly how the place would be furnished. No wheel-back cottagey chairs, no chintz, no gay assortment of coloured cushions. There was no femininity at all about the long low room into which I walked straight from the open door.

I looked first to the left of me where Aunt Maggie now stood near an open fireplace which was just a large inlet in the wall and was made of the same rough stone as the outer walls of the cottage. There was a fire basket flanked by a pair of iron dogs in the aperture. Opposite the fireplace was a long deep brown leather couch holding cushions of the same hue. Behind this, running lengthwise with the room, was a rough refectory table, definitely handmade, and well made at that. Even my cursory glance took in this fact. The wall opposite to me had been boarded halfway along its length, and this was topped by a shelf on which stood, at intervals, three wooden animals: a horse, a fox and a dog. The dog was a perfect replica of a Labrador. Aware that my Aunt Maggie was watching me intensely, as was the girl, I turned and looked towards my right. In the middle of a wall which was entirely stark stone, there was another door which led into, I could see beyond, a kitchen. To each side of me, and flanking the front door, were two windows. They were square and rather high, and the sills were the same thickness as the stone.

'Like it?'

Aunt Maggie's question startled me for a moment and I repeated her words 'Like it?' Then I answered, 'I think it's amazing – out—' I had been about to say 'out of this world' but I checked myself in time. It would have been a trite summing up, an easy summing up. I often become annoyed at myself for lazy expression, for not translating my thoughts into meaningful words, and this cottage – this house – this setting deserved meaningful words.

'Where are the stairs?' My Aunt Maggie was bending down slightly towards the girl now.

With a skipping movement that had about it the jerky abandoned style of a child at play, the girl went towards the other doorway, and we followed.

The kitchen I saw was for use as a kitchen and nothing else. It held a Calor gas stove and a shallow stone sink above which there was a Calor water heater. On one side of the sink was a draining board; on the other, a small table. Beyond this, there was a door which doubtless opened into a pantry. On the wall opposite the stove and the sink was another door, which evidently led outside. And next to this, sprouting almost vertically out of the room, were the stairs.

The sight of their steepness had almost silenced Aunt Maggie. Except for a noise that was a cross between 'Oh!' and a groan she made no verbal comment, and bringing her eyes from the dim tunnel of the staircase she looked at me. Then, being Aunt Maggie, she smiled, although somewhat wryly.

'Shall we try it?' she asked.

My lips at least were smiling as I said, 'I'll go first,' but before I had finished speaking the girl was in front of me and she ascended by the simple method of using both her hands and feet.

I disdained to follow her example, at least for the first four stairs, but before I had reached the twelfth and final stair, I had resorted to her sensible means of going up this particular stairway. There was no landing, and, as I stepped out of the well of the stairs straight into a room, I did not look about me but turned swiftly and, bending forward, held out my hand to assist Aunt Maggie.

But my help was disdainfully thrust aside, not by my aunt's hands, she was using those as I had done, but by her voice, saying, 'Don't fluster me else I'll be over.'

I had never looked upon my Aunt Maggie as old – she was an ageless creature. Some days she appeared thirty or younger, at least in her outlook, and, physically, never over fifty. But, as she pulled herself up into the room and I put out my hand to steady her, I thought – this is going to try her – and I remembered that Aunt Maggie was sixty-five. Yet, when she straightened up, her breathing was even and she seemed undisturbed.

We moved away from the unprotected well of the staircase as if afraid of becoming overbalanced, then we looked around the room. It was the lowness of the ceiling that I noticed first; it was not more than six feet high. A tall person would have had to stoop. I am five feet seven and I felt that my hair was almost scraping it. There was one window in this room, small and square like those downstairs. Under it was a single wooden bed covered with a thick plaid travelling rug. There was a chest of drawers against the wall at the foot of the bed, and on the top of them was a small swing mirror. On the wall opposite was a long oak plain wardrobe like a detached cupboard; and, between the two walls, a door led into another room.

The girl went first. When we followed I found that the same pattern was repeated here; a single bed, a chest of drawers, a mirror and a wardrobe; no facilities for washing. The question did cross my mind at that moment. Not – is there a bathroom? I hadn't expected that. But – was there an indoor lavatory? And where did we wash and bathe? These questions were to be answered when we returned downstairs, but my attention was drawn now to yet another staircase, or, to be more explicit, a ladder placed straight against the wall and leading to a hatch in the low ceiling. When I looked up towards it, then down again, it was to find the girl's eyes fastened on mine. I could see she wanted to speak, so I waited.

What she said was straight to the point. 'That's mine.' She pointed upwards.

'Yours?' I inclined my head towards her. 'You sleep here?'

She shook her head from side to side vigorously. 'Just play – my toys up there – I sleep with Grannie.'

'Oh!' I glanced swiftly at Aunt Maggie. She wasn't looking at me, but at the girl, and, when the girl turned towards her, they smiled at each other.

The girl leading the way again, we descended to the ground floor. I think it was more awkward getting down the stairs than going up. I went face forward but Aunt Maggie, being more sensible, returned the way she had come, using her hands and her feet.

In the kitchen once more, dusting her palms against each other, Aunt Maggie remarked, 'There's going to be some washing of hands around here if nothing else. Which reminds me—' She looked from me to the girl and asked on a little laugh, 'is there a bathroom of sorts?'

The girl answered Aunt Maggie's laugh with one of her own which was again of a high squeaking quality exactly like that of an excited child, and, opening the back door, she pointed to the wall. There, hanging on a nail, was a long zinc bathtub.

The girl was already running down a roughly paved path to some bushes, amongst which stood a sentry-like structure.

The twinkle was deep in Aunt Maggie's eyes as she

turned to me and said, 'It's been known to freeze up around here in November!'

'We needn't stay that long.' I was thinking with nostalgia, but only for a moment, of the beautiful sanitary arrangements in our house in Eastbourne, but as Aunt Maggie said airily, 'Aw, well, sufficient unto the day . . . ' I thought, yes, sufficient unto the day. What did sanitary arrangements matter anyway? So close had I become entwined in my surroundings within a matter of not more than fifteen minutes, that had Aunt Maggie said anything detrimental about the amenities of the cottage I would have resented it as a personal affront.

I turned and went into the kitchen and opened the pantry door. It was dim and very cool. It went quite a way back with shelves all around it; opposite to me was a marble slab on which stood a large brown loaf, two bottles of milk, and a round of butter with an acorn pattern on the top. There was some tinned food on one of the shelves and a number of empty screw-top jars.

Aunt Maggie, coming to the door and looking past me towards the bread and butter, exclaimed, 'Well, that'll give us a start.' She narrowed her eyes as she spoke. Then she exclaimed, 'I've not seen butter done like that for years. Well, now we can get settled in.'

Aunt Maggie turned away and I was about to do the same when the girl almost overbalanced us both as she pushed past us into the larder and, reaching to the far corner of the marble slab, she grabbed up two china mugs. They looked like Coronation mugs, but I couldn't see what was written on them because, like the book, she held them tightly pressed to her chest. Then, looking at me she said, 'Mine 'n' Davie's.'

I had a picture of the bride's hand waving out of the car window calling 'Davie' and the name put my teeth on edge – I had already associated the name Davie with the surname McVeigh. It didn't need much stretching of the imagination to know where the designation 'Mad' came in. But what had this Davie – Davie McVeigh – to do with the cottage? A little tentative quizzing might enlighten me and I was about to proceed with it when the girl, now standing by the kitchen table and still holding the mugs, jerked her head upright and appeared to listen. So definite was her attitude that both Aunt Maggie and I listened with her. We could hear nothing, but the girl now moved swiftly to the kitchen door and stood on the stone slab outside, her head still cocked to one side. Then we heard what she had heard, the sound which made her turn and run like a deer, past us again, through the kitchen, through the living room and out onto the path that led through the copse. I had just reached the door when I saw the pink flash of her dress among the trees.

'That was a whistle.'

I turned to Aunt Maggie. 'Yes, but from quite a distance away.'

'You don't think it was from the house?'

'No.' I shook my head.

The whistle had been thin and high, like notes from a reed pipe. I turned my gaze from my aunt and looked down the gentle slope to the lake as I said, 'I once saw a shepherd in Spain playing on a pipe that sounded like that.'

I had said I had 'seen' the shepherd; but I had never seen him; he had been miles away in the hills.

I went out and walked towards the car, amazement filling me. I had spoken of Spain, I had spoken about the shepherd. I hadn't mentioned the name of the man who had told me that the pipe I was then hearing was being played miles away in the hills, but he had been in my consciousness and he had remained there for some seconds without causing me panic. I stopped and looked back at the stone cottage. Already it seemed to be working, already its calm strength was oozing into me.

I began to unpack the car rapidly, carrying the heaviest cases into the house, making two journeys to each one of Aunt Maggie's, aware all the time that she was covertly watching me. It didn't matter. Aunt Maggie was always watching me. Well, she could watch me now getting better. I couldn't wait to get settled in.

CHAPTER TWO

It was seven o'clock and Aunt Maggie and I were sitting in two rather decrepit deck-chairs outside the cottage. We had sat in silence for at least fifteen minutes before Aunt Maggie commented for the second time in the past hour, 'You know, I've a good mind to take a dander over.'

'I wouldn't. They're bound to know we're here; the girl would have told them. Anyway, as this is the only place the road leads to, they will know it was us coming down.'

'Yes, that's the funny thing. As you say, they were bound to know it was us. Then why hasn't somebody been across? Poor manners, I should say.'

'At a wedding—' There I had said the word, and I went on boldly, 'there is always so much to do, everybody getting in everybody else's way. You know how it is.' I was looking at the darkening water, but I knew that my Aunt Maggie's eyes were full on me.

It was some minutes before she spoke and then she remarked, 'It was odd that bed being used, wasn't it? You would have thought they would have stripped it after the last tenant. And, then, it being made up with a sleeping-bag – funny.'

Yes, I myself thought it was funny. Underneath the plaid travelling rug, there hadn't been the usual bed-clothes but a home-made sleeping bag, comprised simply of an old eider-down sewn together to form the bag. This was covered inside and out with two sheets which had also been sewn to form bags. Doubtless it was a very easy way to deal with bedding but I couldn't see myself climbing into a sleeping-bag each night. In the far room, which was to be Aunt Maggie's, there were three blankets and two pillows under another travelling rug, but no sheets. The lack of sheets she said wouldn't worry her for that night – she was so tired she could sleep on the grass.

We had come prepared with a lot of tinned food as Miss Cleverly's letter had indicated we were off the beaten track, so, together with the bread and butter from the larder and a tin of tongue and some salad stuff we had bought on the way, we made quite a satisfying meal. Later, as we washed up, Aunt Maggie was so funny about the zinc bath, going to the length of giving a demonstration of how she would get in and out of it, which included slipping on the soap, that I laughed outright.

A quaint silence had followed my unusual burst of merriment, then Aunt Maggie put her arm about me and pressing me to her said, 'I'm going to enjoy myself here.'

What she really meant was – she was going to be happy here because she thought that in this charming oasis I would regain health of both mind and body – and, perhaps, enough self-confidence to enable me to live with my fellow creatures.

Because of my parents, I had lived with distrust from my earliest memories, and this did not engender faith in others. Yet I had lived in faith for one glorious year. But the shattering of my faith for the second time was more destructive than anything my parents had done to me, or maybe I had felt it more keenly because of the quicksand foundation they had laid – I didn't know. At this moment, I didn't want to think. Let the past creep back gradually.

I looked over the lake, and saw a swallow darting in and out of the last rays of the sun as it flickered on the water. He was after his evening meal, and, as he darted and bobbed and twisted, I realized I was setting his motions to the distant sound of music.

'They'll likely be having a dance on the lawn,' said Aunt Maggie. 'Well, if they go on till midnight they won't keep me awake. Once I get my head down I'll be gone.'

'It'll soon be dark,' I said. 'I'd better try lighting that lamp.'

'That's not a bad idea.'

Aunt Maggie hoisted herself out of the chair and, folding it up, carried it and laid it against the wall of the cottage. I did the same with mine, and then we went indoors.

The lamp stood on a side table. It was an old-fashioned one with a pink bowl but it had been converted to take Calor gas. The conversion had been ingeniously achieved by a tube which ran from the bowl down to a junction near the floor boards. There it joined a metal pipe and, so, went to the main tank in the kitchen which reposed in a cupboard under the sink and fed both the water heater and the stove as well. Being so fixed, the lamp was not movable and I had noted that, unless one had very good eyesight, it would be difficult to read sitting comfortably before the fire for the table was some distance from the couch. I probably could manage, but I doubted whether Aunt Maggie would be able to read unless she was sitting directly under the lamp. But, as she had said, all she wanted to do tonight was to get her head down on the pillow.

I had the match lit in my hand and was bending over, my face close to the globe, and was about to cautiously turn on the tap when I was so startled by the door being thrust open that I swung round and almost upset the whole contraption.

'What the blazes!'

Opposite to me stood the man with the odd-coloured hair. He had appeared a big, bulky individual on the road, but now his size seemed to have doubled. He looked enormous, ungainly, crude; there was about him some quality of the rugged stone of which the cottage was built. But the stone of the cottage gave out a warmness; this man did not. His face was not contorted with anger as I had seen it earlier, but now was wide with surprise and what I could only think of as blank amazement tinged with annoyance.

'You two!'

The words were certainly not complimentary in their implication.

'Yes. We two!' My back was stiff and my chin thrust out. I had said 'We two,' but Aunt Maggie was in the kitchen.

'What are you doing here?'

The man took two slow steps towards me and, as he approached, I was overwhelmed with the fear that we had settled in the wrong cottage.

My voice had a weak note as I asked, 'This place is Lowtherbeck, isn't it?'

'Yes, it's Lowtherbeck.'

'Roger's Cross?'
'Roger's Cross – right again.'
'There isn't another cottage about?'
'No. There isn't another cottage, not hereabouts.'
'Well, we've taken this cottage for three months.'
'You?' He screwed up his face. 'We were expecting a Miss Fuller and – and, I understand, her young niece – but not until Monday.'
'I'm Miss Fuller.' Aunt Maggie came slowly from the kitchen. 'I sent Miss Cleverly a wire saying that we were coming today instead of Monday. She had told me previously that the cottage was ready for us at any time.'
The man had not moved his body, but had turned his head and was looking down at Aunt Maggie.
'We didn't get your wire, unless –' He paused. '– unless it got mixed up with the wedding ones.'
'Well, be that as it may, I sent the wire and here we are.'
'Yes, I can see that, and it's damned awkward. My brother was sleeping here tonight; the house is full.'
'Then you'll just have to let him share your room, won't you?' Aunt Maggie's voice was deceptively civil.
'That, again, is going to be slightly awkward, madam.'
'Miss.'
'Miss.'
He turned his big head gravely towards her. 'You see, I sleep here most of the year. When it isn't let, I could say I live here.'
'Miss Cleverly should have explained this in her letter.'
'There was no need. I'm always out before the tenants arrive.'

I watched Aunt Maggie and the man survey each other, weighing up the form as if before combat. And now Aunt Maggie, dropping into old-fashioned prim courtesy as she was at times wont to do, said, 'I don't know whom I have the honour of addressing.'

As the man laughed, I could have lifted my hand and struck him across the mouth so strong was my anger against him.

'You have the honour, Miss – ' he stressed the 'miss' ' – of addressing David Bernard Michael McVeigh.'

'Thank you.' Aunt Maggie seemed to be losing ground. She swallowed, then indicating me with a motion of her hand, she said, 'This is my niece, Mrs Lac—'

I closed my eyes for a second as Aunt Maggie, retracting quickly, changed my name to 'Miss Prudence Dudley.'

When I opened my eyes, the man was looking at me full in the face. I did not expect him to say anything so trivial as 'How do you do' or 'Pleased to meet you', and he didn't.

He said instead, 'Why the devil did you come down the lane?'

Here we went again! My chin moved twice before I replied; then, and not too quietly, I said, 'We were directed to come that way.'

Before McVeigh could make any comment on this, Aunt Maggie put in, 'Why are you pretending you are surprised to see us here? You must have known who we were this afternoon. That road leads nowhere else but to the house up yonder.' She thrust a sharp finger towards the large house.

'There, you are mistaken. There's a turning that

branches off to the right about a quarter of a mile before you reach our place. It connects with the fell road. If you had taken the fell road, you would have come in by that way.'

'Well, we didn't, and we're here, and that's all about it. And I don't think we're answerable to anyone but Miss Cleverly.'

'Really?' There was question in the word.

'Yes, really! I made arrangements to take the cottage through a Miss Cleverly and I will continue to do business with her – perhaps, you'll enlighten me—' Aunt Maggie was back on the pedantic line again. 'Where do you come in on all this?'

'Me?' He was pointing to his chest where I could see the muscles bulging under a starkly white shirt. 'Oh, me. I only happen to be the owner of the set-up.'

I swallowed dryly. Aunt Maggie swallowed. I clasped and unclasped my hands as my mind repeated again and again: oh, no, no.

It seemed a long time before I heard Aunt Maggie ask in a slightly subdued tone, 'Who, then, is Miss Cleverly?'

'That will take a lot of explaining, Miss Fuller.' There was a trace of sardonic laughter in his voice now. 'Miss Cleverly is a lady who runs my house. She fills the position of housekeeper and adviser, and – performs lots of other functions.'

I felt my face turning scarlet. Again, I wanted to take my hand and strike out at the mouth from which the deep cool-sounding words had come. There flashed into my mind the picture of my father's last apartment, and his last mistress – the last one, that is, that I had seen. I was glaring at the man's back now for he had turned round.

As he walked towards the kitchen door, he said over his shoulder, 'I'll collect my bed if you don't mind.'

Aunt Maggie moved across the dim room and stood near me. Under her breath she muttered, 'Don't let him get you down. We'll not see much of him – there'll be no need to. Anyway, if you can't stick him, we'll find some other place.'

Yes, we would certainly have to find someplace else, for I couldn't tolerate that individual. I couldn't put up with David Bernard Michael McVeigh for long without bursting asunder. The man did something to me; he made me want to hit out. It was a terrifying feeling for I had only hit out once in my life before, and then I had been driven to it, and was half-mad.

'There is always a fly in the ointment, lass. That's life.' Aunt Maggie's voice was sad now and this broke my thoughts away from myself; I was now filled with concern for her. She had put up with the long hot journey, even car sickness. She had put a good face on everything, and, not only today, but for years past, she had done everything to smooth the granite edges of life that would from time to time dig at me. Now she sounded tired, and not a little sad. Making an effort, I put out my hand and touched hers and whispered a saying to her she had often extolled in my childhood: 'Big balloons make the loudest bang.'

The balloon appeared at the kitchen door.

'Two mugs that were in the pantry?' the balloon asked.

'The girl took them,' I said.

'The girl?' McVeigh was moving into the room now. Under his arm was the rolled-up sleeping-bag. 'You mean Frannie?'

'I don't know what her name is, but she took them.'

'Oh, well.'

He was standing with his back to the front door, and, through narrowed lids, he looked first at Aunt Maggie and then at me – his gaze taking in, not only my face, but the whole of me.

His voice slightly mocking, he said, 'Well I suppose it'll sort itself out. Sleep well. I put a clean set – ' he hitched at the bedding under his arm ' – on. You'll find plenty of linen and such in the loft if you require it. Good-night.'

Neither of us answered. And, not until I watched through the window the dark bulk of him disappear in the copse, did I turn to Aunt Maggie.

She was seated now and was silent – her silence disturbed me.

'Let's go to bed,' I suggested. I put my hand on her shoulder.

She turned her head, looked up at me, and remarked, 'So Miss Cleverly is the housekeeper. Well! Well! From her letter, I would have said she was around the same age as myself. Funny, the impressions one gets – the wrong impressions.'

'I don't think you could have got a wrong impression about that individual – shall I light the lamp?'

'No, don't bother. If we have a good sleep, we'll see things differently tomorrow, be able to laugh at life again, eh?' My aunt patted my hand where it still rested on her shoulder. Then, with an endearing movement, she lowered her cheek towards it.

These were the moments in my life when I knew that deep feeling was not dead in me. When I could respond to affection. In this moment I knew I loved my Aunt Maggie very deeply.

The bed was placed in such a position that, when you were sitting propped up, you could see the lake out the window and, because of the added height, over the hill bordering the left side of the water as well to a range of higher hills beyond. I could pick out small details quite clearly because there was moonlight, strong white moonlight, that made the scene almost as clear as it had been in the sunlight.

It was nearing eleven o'clock and I had been in bed for almost two hours but I had not yet been able to approach sleep. In fact, I was much wider awake than I had been when driving in the heat of the day. My mind seemed alert and my thinking was devoid of the slightest trace of panic, which was strange to me, especially as my thoughts were delving into the past. It was the moonlight that had done it.

When I had first come to bed, I had been thinking of our visitor. It was odd, but I hated to think of him as the owner of the cottage, yet I found, as I continued to gaze down into the lake where the moon was buried fathoms deep, and watched its light softly dimming now and again as a cloud raced across its surface, that I was forgetting the man. At least, my anger against him had subsided. He was, in this moment, washed of all importance; his rudeness had not the power to anger me any more, and it seemed that it would never again have such influence – he just didn't matter. Yet it was because of the feeling he had aroused in me, the feeling of retaliation, that my mind had slowly sunk back into the past, the not so very distant past, until it reached the point where, for the first time in my life, I had lifted my hands with the intent to hurt another; I had been incensed to the point where I was struggling madly with a man – with my husband.

There was a contraction of the nerves of my stomach now. My mind skirted round the thought of violence and moved quickly away – further back – to the time when I had lain in the bedroom of my Aunt Maggie's house and peopled the empty house opposite with characters. That was until the day when the real characters took over.

A family, as I've said before, came to live in the house. The daughter was at college. When she came home and heard there was a sick girl lying in the room that she could see from her bedroom window, she came to visit me. With that visit began my friendship with Alice Hornbrook.

Alice was twenty-three. She was what could be called an intellectual. She had just received her degree in English and had secured her first teaching post in Eastbourne. When she learned that I wrote stories, she asked to see them, merely I think out of politeness or to give some comfort to a sick person, but her praise of my work, which I knew to be genuine, acted like an injection of elixir on me.

'You must write, write seriously. Go on with this.' Alice's high, clear voice seemed to come across the lake now. A night bird was calling; it was saying, 'You must go on with this; you must go on with this.'

I did go on with it. I wrote a sixty-thousand-word story which, when Alice read it, she criticized.

'I would rewrite this again,' she told me. 'Make it eighty-thousand, and you'd do well to cut out the chunks of homespun philosophy and bitter passages. There's enough acid in your cynicism to make it a winner.'

I did as she advised, and the day I received a letter from a publisher stating that he would take pleasure in publishing my work and asking if I would come up to town to have a talk, my nervous complaint was cured and I got out of bed.

From this distance, I think my early success was on a par with that of Françoise Sagan. The critics hailed me for my youth while praising me for my knowledge of life, for the cynicism of a professional, for the competence with which I had handled the eternal triangle. But, didn't I know a lot about the eternal triangle? Hadn't I been brought up with it, fed on it from my earliest days? The characters in my books were only thinly disguised replicas of my mother and father, together with the second and third husbands on the one hand, and the numerous mistresses on the other.

I wrote three books in just under two years and I was there – I had arrived. I was selling so well, especially in America, that I need not worry about money ever. And I did not worry about money. That was one thing that had never caused me any anxiety. It seems to me strange at times that people should worry so much about money. If I had not a penny tomorrow, I know it wouldn't worry me; truthfully, it wouldn't.

Alice Hornbrook and I were friends for five years.

She, too, called Aunt Maggie, 'Aunt Maggie'. And I called her mother and father 'Aunt Ann' and 'Uncle Dick'. Ours was that kind of close relationship. Then Alice's uncle came to stay with them. He was young, as he was her mother's youngest brother. His name was Ian Lacey, and from the moment I first looked at him my life was changed. Not that I fell in love with him straightaway; no, I would say that he gradually charmed me into loving him. But, right from the first moment, I was fascinated by him – for, besides his charm, he was amusing, and he was helpless, so helpless that he needed me – at least part of me.

And we had something in common, a strong bond – we were both writers, the only difference being that I had been published and he hadn't. When I say that Ian was helpless, I mean he was helpless with regard to money. He was helpless as a writer. He wanted someone to lean on, to guide him, and, although he was nine years older than I, I felt the elder. I also thought that I was the only one who understood him – had ever understood him, or could ever understand him. Ian indoctrinated me well.

For the first year of our acquaintance, Ian only stayed for short periods with his sister Mrs Hornbrook. But, on these visits, he spent most of the time with me in Aunt Maggie's house, and during this time my own work suffered – if I may use that word to imply neglect. For I would spend days reading and revising his work, or advising him about some story he was concerned with at the moment.

Before Ian took up his abode permanently with his sister in the house across the way, I was aware that it was impossible for him to follow my advice. Put a pen in his hand and a ream of paper on the table and his words flowed. Showy, flowery, verbose words – words resulting in long sentences with obscure meanings. He would spend hours with a dictionary and *Roget's Thesaurus* looking for a glorious ornamental adjective. But his prolixity did not cause me to withdraw my help, or lessen the love I then had for him.

On the night that Alice came to tell me that she was going to marry a schoolmaster (this came as something of a shock, for I wasn't even aware that she was interested in a man; she didn't seem the mating type, and never discussed the male) – it was on that night that Alice asked me, 'You're not getting serious about Ian, are you?'

For answer, I said, 'Is there any reason why I shouldn't?'

And to this she shook her head as she replied, 'No. Only that he's unstable; he's never been able to hold down a job in his life. Ian was the youngest, and my grandmother spoiled him. When she died, she passed on the task to her four daughters, and now it'll be up to a wife to complete the course. You want to think seriously about it. And, by the way,' Alice had nodded sagely, 'don't waste your good time on his stuff – he'll never be able to write in a month of Sundays. And Ian's kind can become as jealous as hell of another's success.'

I had said somewhat bitterly, 'You seem to love your uncle.'

Alice answered, 'I'm very fond of you and would hate to see you hurt.'

'Is that all you have got against Ian?'

She had considered for a moment, and then had said rather doubtfully, 'Yes. Yes, that's all.'

Many months later, when I recalled this conversation, I knew that Alice had spoken the truth when she said that was all she knew.

But at that time, when Aunt Maggie spoke along lines similar to Alice's, I began to think, and I knew I must get away and sort things out in my own mind. I did not want my marriage to repeat my mother and father's life all over again. I felt that if my marriage went on the rocks it would surely kill me – I had enough experience of marriages going wrong. So I went away and thought things out, and I came to the conclusion that my parents' marriage had broken up because neither of them needed the other sufficiently. Ian needed me. He might be weak, but was that a great fault? My father wasn't weak, he was strong, and look what he had done to himself and to others. My decision was – if Ian wanted me to, I would marry him . . .

I waited and waited, but Ian didn't mention marriage. Then, one night, the situation, which was becoming emotionally unbearable for me, was brought to a head. It was the night I told Ian that I was going on a tour with Aunt Maggie and might be away for two months or more. At that moment, he seemed to have become hysterical – I wasn't to leave him, he needed me. How was he to exist without me?

I had never felt so happy in my life. I consoled him, saying I would never leave him – we would be married and go touring ourselves. Aunt Maggie would understand.

It was one of the awful blows to my pride when later he reminded me that he had never mentioned marriage to me, it was I who had done the proposing. And, dear God, how true that had been!

Ian and I were married in the autumn and we spent our honeymoon in Spain. It was then that I had heard the thin whistle of the pipe which was like the sound that had made Frannie run to answer the call today. When we returned to England, we stayed, at her request, with Aunt Maggie. She said she would be lonely without us. That I am sure was a lie for my benefit – Aunt Maggie sensed disaster.

And disaster came early in the year, in the form of a letter from Wales. In an old magazine, a woman had seen the picture of a man boarding a plane with the authoress Prudence Dudley. The caption stated that the man was Prudence Dudley's husband. She wanted to know if there was some mistake because the man, she felt sure, was her own husband, and the father of their two children, one aged three and the other seven. He had deserted her three years ago.

My mind had now reached a point where I was fighting with a man, with Ian, going for him like a savage wild creature as if with intent to kill. And I think that had been my purpose, for when, in his easygoing, charming fashion, he admitted the contents of this woman's letter to be true, I did go mad for a time.

The Hornbrooks were devastated by the turn of events. Our association naturally was broken. I could not bear Alice's sympathy for her eyes seemed to say 'I told you so.' Although she had not known the facts of her uncle's life, from her estimation of his character, she had made a pretty shrewd guess.

When the case was brought to court, the newspapers did not hesitate to make top-line news of it. I had felt very ill during all that time, ill and dazed, and, if it hadn't been for Aunt Maggie, I think I would have ended my life. But it was nearly ended in a natural way by the premature birth of my baby. From the moment I knew that I wasn't Ian's legal wife, there had arisen in me a horrible distaste for the child I was carrying, and when, three months ago, it was prematurely stillborn I knew a measure of relief. But the relief was very short-lived, for in its place came a deep sense of guilt – I felt I had killed the child – I had wished it out of existence.

After the disastrous birth of the baby, I lay in a dark, muddled kind of numbness for weeks. I was back in the state of 'nerves' that had hit me once before. Once more, I was retreating from myself, or, more true to say, I was dragging myself from contact with life – unbearable life.

Again, it was Aunt Maggie, and only she, who pulled me back to the surface of living. Now, here I was, my head just breaking water. I was looking about me realizing that I was a free agent. I could do what I liked, go where I liked – stay put where I liked, and write, write again. The thought of writing again brought back the thought of Ian. Ian's last words to me had been, 'No matter what you think, I love you – above all I need you.'

I didn't know so much about the love, Ian's kind of love was worthless anyway, but I did know quite a lot about the need. Ian had needed me all right, he had needed me to support his ego, for he was a writer who couldn't write, at least, except for his own enjoyment, to satisfy his taste for words, elaborate words. Well, he had plenty of time to ponder over words now. He would have enough food for thought in prison.

Prison! I looked out onto the moonlight-swept scene before me – the wide, wild, free scene, and, for the first time since the sentence of six months' imprisonment had been passed on him, I realized the awfulness of his punishment; after all, his crime had been weakness, breaking the law through weakness. At this moment, he was encased in a cell, perhaps lying there thinking as I was. I was amazed at the voice in my head which said, 'Poor Ian.' Yet I knew at the same time that, if I lived to be a hundred, I did not want to set eyes again on the man who had played husband to me.

I told myself I must stop thinking, I must go to sleep. But I didn't go to sleep; I lay looking out of the window across the water, the Little Water. It was really a charming name for the lakes – the Lil Water and the Big Water, the girl had said. Did the Big Water lie within the grounds too? This thought directed my mind to the house along the hill path. The music and the noise had died down some time ago. Perhaps the guests were indoors now continuing the jollification, as Aunt Maggie would have termed it.

As if in denial of their presence indoors, there came to me now the sound of laughter, the mingled laughter of men and women. It rose and fell as if being carried by the wind, or it may have been the laughter of people running. I sat up straighter in the bed and turned my head round so that my eyes could take in the black blur that was the thicket. The moon was shining on the top of it, but the side of it was casting a deep shadow and, under my widening gaze, there came running out of the shadow a number of people – six or eight – I didn't know how many at first. They were laughing and talking. One figure that had been carrying a basket of some kind ran to the edge of the lake and, after dropping the basket onto the ground, he began leaping madly about.

Someone shouted, 'Look at Alec!'

The leaping figure now stopped and caught hold of a girl and waltzed her madly over the grass. When he stopped, the girl fell over and lay laughing wildly. The man called Alec shouted, 'Give us a jig, Peter.'

A member of the party who stood by the lakeside swaying gently as if rocked by the breeze brought his hands upwards and began to play what looked like a small concertina. The air became filled with the strains of a Highland reel accompanied by shouts and whoops from the rest of the party.

'Here we go – upsy-daisy!'

'Yipp–ee!'

'Oh! me boys; Oh! me boys of Barrow-in-Furness!'

The laughter was loud now, wild-sounding.

I was kneeling on the bed gazing downwards. I flicked my eyes around as I heard Aunt Maggie shuffling into the room.

'Well, this is too much – it's beyond a joke.'

'Were you asleep?'

'I was dead to the world. The sound frightened the life out of me for a moment. They're all mad drunk.'

'They're certainly not sober.'

'I wish I could see that McVeigh, I'd give him the

length of my tongue. Look! look!' Aunt Maggie was kneeling on the bed beside me now. 'It's like a witches' Sabbath. There's two of them dancing in the water. Well, they can dance where they like, but they're not doing it here at this time of night – we've rented this place.'

She had pulled open the window before I could stop her but with the sharp command of 'No! Aunt Maggie,' I prevented her from calling out. 'Let them alone. In their present mood, you don't know what they'd do. They might come in here or—'

My voice trailed off and my eyes turned in the direction of the copse, for there, coming to a halt on the edge of the moonlight, I saw the tall thin figure of a young man. His hair looked black and his face very white and he was biting on his lip as he smiled. Then, apparently hearing a noise that was not distinguishable to us because of the music, singing, and shouting, he cast a glance over his shoulder. As if the man had been conjured out of the shadow itself, there stood Mr David Bernard Michael McVeigh! I found that, ironically, I was giving him his full title when I thought of him. I saw him grab at the dark man's arm and point; then I watched the young man pull himself away, apparently giving an angry retort.

I kept well back from the window, indicating to Aunt Maggie to do the same. The two men were now standing near the corner of the cottage and some of their words were audible.

I recognized McVeigh's voice saying, 'I told you to keep them clear of here.'

The dark man's immediate answer was lost to me, but I noted that his tone sounded angry; and, then his voice rose and I heard the words: 'You try telling Alec anything when he's on the bottle.'

'That crowd should never have been asked in the first place. I was against it – I told you.'

'You're always against some damn thing – your life is made up of being against things.'

'Look!' McVeigh's voice was deep and low, and I found myself bending forward to catch the words. 'I don't want any trouble with you tonight, Roy. Let the wedding day end in peace.'

'Huh! You're the one to talk about peace!'

'Now, look.' The voice was brittle. 'If you want to take up where we left off, it's all the same to me, but first I'll get this lot away from here.'

McVeigh's head looked as silver as the moonlight as I watched it move towards the man with the concertina. The music stopped abruptly, but the dancers, still laughing and yelling, continued their capers for some seconds before their laughter petered out in spluttering and coughing.

The night returned to its serenity for a second before the ringleader Alec shouted, 'Aw, Davie, man, why d'ya stop it? Come on, come on and fling it! Hoots! Toots! an' a drop o' the hard!'

'Be quiet, Alec.'

'Aw, man, it's a weddin' night. Come on, let your hair down.'

'I've told you—'

The rest of the words were lost, but I knew that McVeigh was telling them that the cottage was occupied for I saw a number of faces turn in our direction.

Then Alec's voice rose again, not so loud this time, but quite recognizable: 'Well, you said yourself they were stinkers, didn't you? "Prudence by name and prudence by nature" – that's what you said – so why worry? I don't give a damn, Davie man.' The words were slower now. 'It's a weddin' night and nobody should go to bed 'cept those concerned.'

There was a great shout of laughter at this quip. And my hand was moving forward to close the window when the man's next words caught and held my attention.

'Why are you doin' the considerate landlord stunt now, when earlier on you said they were a fossilized pair – the old 'un talkin' like Queen Victoria herself?' he shouted.

'Be quiet, I tell you.'

'Now, Davie, don't tell me what t'do – you know it won't work, not with me it won't.' The voice was menacing one moment, then gay the next. The man now cried: 'Come on, let's have a singsong . . . the one about Pru. How did it go?

Oh Prudence, dear one, take this ring,
And wear it near your heart—'

As the man's voice rang out high over the lake, I saw the silver-headed figure spring forward, only to be stopped by a number of arms. I saw the man retreating towards the water singing tauntingly as he went:

'And give me but one word of hope
Ere I this night depart.'

Aunt Maggie and I exchanged glances, mine indignant, hers surprised. Then we were looking down towards the edge of the lake again. There seemed to be a number of people sprawled about, but McVeigh was standing, and so was the man who had sung the rhyme. I put my hand over my eyes as the fist shot out, yet I seemed to see Alec's feet fly from the ground. I certainly heard the splash as his body hit the water. I kept my eyes covered for two or three minutes, and, when I next raised my head and looked downward, I thought I must have dreamed the whole scene – but for the fact that Aunt Maggie was sitting close to me and was trembling slightly. For the greensward was empty of people; that is, with the exception of two shadows which supported another shadow, and moved into the darkness of the copse. And if I hadn't known that the shadows were two men assisting the drunken brawler whom McVeigh had hit, I might have taken the movement for the swaying of the trees.

'Well, I've seen some things in my time!' Aunt Maggie was shaking her head. 'It didn't seem real, did it?'

When I didn't answer, she patted my arm and said, 'Take no notice of the rhyming; it strikes me the whole lot of them are blind drunk . . . And this – ' she spread wide the palms of her hands ' – and this is the haven of peace. Wait till I see that Miss Cleverly.'

'When you do see her, you can tell her that we are going.'

'Yes. Yes, I will, indeed. There'll be plenty more places to get. It's the end of the season anyway – people will only be too glad to rent cottages or such. There was never a good but there's a better. Well, now – ' she stood up ' – do you think we'll get to sleep after this?'

'We'd better,' I said, 'or we'll be dead beat tomorrow when there'll likely be another long car journey before us.'

'Good-night, lass.'

'Good-night, Aunt Maggie.'

The strangest thing about that strange day was that almost as soon as I lay down again I found myself dropping into sleep, and, as I lost consciousness, I imagined that the scene that had taken place before the lake was part of a dream, and, as sometimes happens in dreams, I desired to continue dreaming, but I didn't.

I must have slept soundly until the next morning, when I was awakened, not only by the smell of frying bacon, but by Aunt Maggie standing over me shaking me gently, saying, 'There's somebody moving about downstairs – and can you smell that?'

Slowly I pulled myself upwards in the bed and blinked the sleep from my eyes – then I sniffed. Following this, I looked up at Aunt Maggie.

'Peace offering from the lord of the clan, I suppose,' Aunt Maggie was whispering down at me.

'You mean *he* is cooking the breakfast?' I was whispering back.

'Who else? And we hadn't any bacon with us. It's going to be awkward giving someone the length of your tongue when they are handing you a plateful of bacon and eggs, isn't it?' Aunt Maggie's eyebrows were now straining towards her hairline.

I swung my legs out of the bed, slipped my feet into slippers, and grabbed up a dressing-gown. As I zipped it up to the neck, I said flatly, 'I never eat breakfast.'

Tricky as it was I descended the staircase face

forward; I was not going to give Mr McVeigh food for laughter by presenting him with a view of my rear.

When I stepped into the kitchen, the frying pan was on the stove. There was steam from hot water in the sink, and on the side table were two trays set most tastefully for breakfast.

My back stiff again, my chin up, I moved into the sitting-room, and there the wind was completely taken out of my sails, for I was not confronted by McVeigh holding out the velvet glove, but by a stranger. She was a woman well into her sixties – as old, I should say, as Aunt Maggie. She was extremely thin, of medium height, and had abundant brown hair without a streak of grey in it. But the face that I saw in profile, first one side then the other, as she darted about the far end of the room was extremely lined.

I knew that she was aware of my presence for some time before she gave the false start, saying, 'Oh! Oh, my! Well, you're up now.'

She came towards me, her step almost on the point of a run, and, when she was standing opposite me, she looked up into my face and smiled, saying, 'I let you lie, you had had a long journey yesterday. And, oh, I am sorry about the place not being ready. You see, I didn't get your wire – it got among the wedding ones, and half of them weren't read, what with one thing and another, you know?'

The woman had almond-shaped eyes – they had been very beautiful at one time – and these had widened at me as she had asked, 'You know?'

Then she went on, 'And not a flower in the place,

and it like a pigsty. Davie – you know Davie? – he sleeps here at times, and you know what men are. You know?' Again the eyes widened with the question. 'And you see I never knew a thing about it – I mean that you were here or anything till they brought Alec Bradley in and then it all came out. They said they hadn't told me because it would fuss me – fuss me, indeed! As if I couldn't cope – oh, good-morning.'

She was now holding her head on one side and looking beyond me to Aunt Maggie. Like a gramophone that was wound up and wouldn't stop until it ran down naturally, she went on, 'You're Miss Fuller? Yes, I can see you're Miss Fuller, and this is your niece. I've been telling her everything. I'm so sorry, but things will be quiet and peaceful after this, dead as a doornail you might say. Nothing much happens here. But it was the wedding. You know?'

I moved aside to let Miss Cleverly get into the kitchen and I was now abreast of Aunt Maggie. As we looked at each other, I knew we were both thinking the same thing: that no matter in what capacity Miss Flora Cleverly served David Bernard Michael McVeigh, it certainly was not that of his mistress.

'Now, your breakfasts are ready. You could have them out on the lawn. It's warm enough and nobody will disturb you.' She turned and wagged her finger at us. 'I promise you that. There's bacon and egg and fried bread and mushrooms. I've brought a couple of bottles of milk over; we have our own milk. We run seven cows, sheep and chickens, and a few pigs, but we go in for mushrooms, you know.'

'It's very kind of you – ' my Aunt Maggie had moved forward ' – but you shouldn't have done this.'

'No trouble. No trouble at all. All in a day's work.' She was moving quickly here and there as she spoke, mashing the tea, turning the toast. She worked with the sure precision of a robot and seemed to be drawing on a store of energy that would never go dry. That was really the thing that struck me immediately about Flora Cleverly – her outstanding energy.

'We are—' Aunt Maggie hesitated. 'I'm slightly at sea with regards to who's who about here. I understand that Mr McVeigh owns the place.'

'Yes, yes, that's right. The one you met – Davie. He's the eldest – he owns Lowtherbeck and what's left of the land, not fifty acres now. It used to run into thousands – would you believe that? Yes – ' she nodded her head at me ' – it was a wonderful estate at one time. Still, we're thankful for what we've got – we must be thankful.'

'Are there other McVeighs?' Aunt Maggie's head was inclined to one side with gentle enquiry.

'There's Roy – he's three years younger than Davie. A nice boy, Roy. That's all that's left of the McVeighs. But we have young Janie with us. It was her sister, Doris, who was married yesterday. They're cousins of the McVeighs.'

'Are you a relative, too?'

For the first time Flora Cleverly's hands ceased their moving and she looked down at them for a moment before she answered Aunt Maggie.

Then, on a laugh she said, 'No. It's funny I'm not, but I've been connected with them all my life.

I brought up the two boys after their mother died, and I've always run the house and seen to everything. When Davie was away I ran the whole place, and everything went on just the same. I've run it now on my own – that is, I mean the house – for thirty-two years. But I ran it even before that, because Mrs McVeigh was never very healthy – I mean strong. There, I mustn't talk any more, you must have your breakfast. I've brought you over a piece of lamb and some vegetables for your dinner.' She thumbed in the direction of the pantry. 'And if you will, we'd be pleased to see you at tea – there's so much to be eaten up,' she added. 'And after that you can settle down and only see us when you want to. But, if you're short, you've just got to ask – I'm nearly always sure to have what you want; I've always kept a good larder. There, now.'

With an oven cloth she whisked the hot plates one after the other out of the oven onto the trays and we lifted them up and followed her into the living-room.

'Would you like to have breakfast on the porch?' I asked Aunt Maggie.

'Yes, that would be nice.'

Even as I spoke, Miss Cleverly had lifted the table into position and brought forward a couple of chairs.

'There now, you're all set. Don't forget what I told you – anything you want.'

She was standing on the threshold of the door when I asked, 'Who is the little girl we saw here yesterday?'

'Oh, you mean Frannie? She's from across the hill. She lives with her grannie on the road to Brookfield.

But she's always about here, has been from when she was a child. We couldn't get rid of her if we wanted to. The boys have sort of adopted her, you know. Quite daft over the boys she was.'

'How old is she?' asked Aunt Maggie.

'Coming up sixteen. It's a pity, isn't it?'

'Has she always been like that?' I asked softly.

'Oh, no, no. It happened one day on the Big Water. That's the other lake, you know.'

It seemed that whenever Miss Cleverly used the words 'you know' in either the form of a statement or a question she accompanied them by a widening of her almond-shaped eyes. It was an odd co-ordination.

'They were all out in a boat,' she continued, 'her father and mother and her. They were always quarrelling, the pair of them, and he must have hit her – he was a jealous man – and the boat capsized. And that must have been that. Their bodies were never recovered – the Big Water's very deep in the middle – but the child was found lying, late that night, floating face up in the reeds. They thought she was dead at first, but she was just unconscious, must have been like that from the time she hit the water, and that saved her. Anyway, whatever it was, when she pulled round, well, she was like she is now. She's never developed. It's a pity, isn't it?'

Both my Aunt Maggie and I nodded slowly in assent. Yes, indeed, it was a pity.

'Now eat your breakfasts. I'll be seeing you at tea.'

With that, Miss Cleverly left us abruptly.

There had been a matron at my boarding-school who used to speak in the same manner. Eat your breakfast, do your nails, tidy your room. I felt like a child again.

Aunt Maggie cut into her bacon, but before she conveyed the piece to her mouth she leaned across to me and said quietly, 'Variety is the spice of life.' Then, with an effort, she smothered her laughter.

CHAPTER THREE

The day should have passed peaceably enough. The sun was hot again, but not so fierce as the day before, just comfortable enough to lie in, and that's what I was doing. I was lying on the green slope near the lake while Aunt Maggie lay in a deck-chair higher up in the shade. Earlier in the day, I had sampled the water but, to my disappointment, I found I could not stay in it very long for the temperature was almost freezing.

Together, Aunt Maggie and I had made lunch, eaten it, and washed up. Now, to all appearances, we were relaxed. Aunt Maggie might be, but I certainly wasn't. I was all keyed up inside waiting for Aunt Maggie to say, 'Well, isn't it time to make a move?' If there had been anyone to send with a message, I would have certainly sent a note with our excuses, for I didn't want to listen to apologies about last night – the rhyme was still running in my head. Thinking along these lines, I found I was wishing that the girl Frannie would make her appearance, but no one disturbed us.

And then Aunt Maggie's voice came at me saying, 'Psst!'

I rolled over on my face, my hands under my chin, and looked at her. Aunt Maggie was sitting straight up now and pointing towards the copse. She wagged her finger while she mouthed silently: 'Someone coming.' I swung round and sat up, supporting myself with my hands, and waited, my gaze directed towards the hill rising from the far shore of the lake.

'I hope I'm not disturbing you?'

The pleasant voice brought me from my studied pose, and I saw, standing a few yards from Aunt Maggie's chair, the young man whom I had seen last night in the moonlight, the one who argued with McVeigh.

'No, no, not in the least,' said Aunt Maggie.

'I'm – I'm Roy McVeigh and I've come to fetch you over.'

The man was looking across towards me now and, as I rose slowly to my feet, I saw that his eyes, like those of his brother last night, were taking me all in. But there was no covert insolence in his face – interest, perhaps, and, if I had felt inclined to search for compliments, I might have said, some admiration. The fabric of the sun-suit I was wearing had an orange-and-yellow pattern on a white background and was an attractive thing in itself.

'This is my niece, Miss Dudley,' said Aunt Maggie.

'How do you do?'

We each inclined our heads slightly to the other. Then I said, 'I won't be a moment.'

'That's all right. There's no hurry.' Roy smiled, a wide easy smile. I did not return it, but moved away and went indoors where I changed the sun-suit for a white linen dress that was deceptively simple. I brushed my hair, noting, as I always did when I looked in the mirror now, that there were single grey hairs among the dark brown ones. I applied a lipstick. That was all. I suppose I was fortunate in having a skin that didn't require much make-up.

When I appeared on the lawn, the young man's eyes again moved over me. After a space, during which Aunt Maggie heaved herself up out of the chair with his assistance, Roy looked at me and said, 'It's nice having people in the cottage again.'

'Do you have many here?' Aunt Maggie was straightening her skirt.

'No, not often; not for long leases.' He smiled. 'Perhaps two or three lots a year, for a week or so. It isn't everybody's cup of tea you know, stuck out in the wilds.'

'It suits us,' Aunt Maggie now turned to me and added, 'will I go and change?'

'That looks quite all right,' I said.

'Oh, please, don't dress up for us. Wait until you see our set-up. It's rough and ready, I can assure you.'

'Ah well and good then. That suits me.'

Aunt Maggie moved towards the copse; Roy waited until I was abreast of her, then he walked by my side and I found he did not disturb me one way or another. He made no mention of last night, leaving that to his brother I supposed.

The 'set-up', as Roy McVeigh had called it, was homely and comfortable, yet, over-all, there was a shabbiness that spoke of hard wear. Like the treads in the carpet on the stairs the curtains, chair covers and cushions looked as if they hadn't been renewed for several years. Although the curtains on the windows were thick and lined, their colour, except where the big old-fashioned curtain rings caught them, was drab beige, but the material near the rings indicated that they may at one time have been blue or green. Yet the room we were sitting in was definitely a drawing-room. There were a number of small tables, two of which I noticed were Louis Quinze and probably authentic antiques. Then there was a china cabinet holding odd pieces of Wedgwood and Spode; and, lastly, a large deep old-fashioned suite of furniture in faded red moquette.

Flora Cleverly was presiding at the tea table, her hands darting over a two-handled Sheffield silver tray holding an ornamental tea service of the same design, all brightly polished. To her side were two cake stands and a small table laden with eatables. Beside Miss Cleverly, Roy McVeigh and ourselves, the only other person in the room was Janie Slater.

Janie was ten and her face had a similar expression to that of her sister when she had looked at me from the back window of the car the day before. But, as yet, Janie didn't get much chance to talk. *'Hand Miss Dudley the sandwiches, Janie. Pass the sugar to Miss Fuller.'* Do this. Do that. See to this. See to that. I could almost see Miss Cleverly's brain at work, organizing, docketing, thinking, thinking ahead to tomorrow when it would organize, reorganize and docket again. Miss Cleverly also did the talking. Her conversation took the form of questions which were mostly addressed to Aunt Maggie, but, as I sat trying to think of something to say to the shy child beside me, Miss Cleverly addressed me pointedly for the first time.

'And what are you? I mean, in what line of business?'

My head had turned sharply towards her and,

whatever answer I might have given, I certainly wouldn't have told her the truth, for I knew what disclosure could mean – even in out-of-the-way places. Dead manuscripts pressed on you to be read. *'When you have a minute, you know.'* But I hadn't a chance to say anything – Aunt Maggie was there before me.

'My niece is the writer Prudence Dudley.'

She didn't say '*a* writer', but '*the* writer'. I knew my face had gone a deep pink; I was also aware that Flora Cleverly had never heard of the writer Prudence Dudley, but that Roy McVeigh had.

So it was he who spoke first, exclaiming, 'Good gracious! Yes, yes, of course, I remember seeing your photograph.' He stopped, embarrassed when it came to him just where he had seen my photograph.

'Davie makes up rhymes. He makes up funny ones.'

Janie, speaking for the first time, was silenced almost immediately. 'Be quiet, Janie! Here, hand Miss Dudley the cake. Well now, to think you're a writer.'

Miss Cleverly did not look at me, all her attention was directed towards the tea-tray, but she went on talking to me. 'We're honoured. We've never had a writer stay before, a painter, yes – two painters and a singer. We certainly knew we had the singer – he practised morning, noon and night. He even had the piano carted over. Oh, yes, we knew all about having a singer, but we've never had a writer – well, now!'

It was at this moment that the door opened and Davie McVeigh came in. Automatically, I sat up straighter on the couch, thinking, Yes, Davie makes up rhymes all right. He was wearing a white shirt and riding breeches. It was evident he had left his top boots outside for on his feet were a pair of old red slippers. His shirt was buttoned at the neck and wrists. I remember noticing this because Roy's shirt was open at the neck and his sleeves were short. One of the men looked free, and the other encased. Now Roy spoke to his brother as if there had never been any harsh words between them.

'What do you think, Davie? This is Miss Prudence Dudley the writer.'

'Yes, I know.' The voice was calm. The big head was turned in my direction; the man was looking down at me, his eyes smiling quite pleasantly. His face had no aggressiveness in it at this moment.

'You know? How do you know? You couldn't have known.' This was Miss Cleverly, her hands still now as she stared towards Davie McVeigh.

'I know because I happen to read now and again. It may be surprising to you, Flora – ' the sarcasm was back in the voice so the man was more recognizable ' – but I do read at times. The cottage is made for reading. I think Miss Dudley – ' he glanced at me ' – will discover that.' After some seconds of silence, he turned and, facing me, said, 'By the way, I never managed to read your second book but I read the first and the third. I liked the third best. Less harsh, more compassionate, if you'll allow me to say so.'

People, I noticed, always added, 'if you'll allow me to say so' after making some cutting criticism. Yet I knew that what he had said was true. I had softened a lot by the time I had written my third book. I also knew that I was pleased, and surprised, that this objectionable man had read my books.

'I don't believe you could have known anything about it.' We were all looking at Flora Cleverly again. 'If you had known she was – *the* Miss Dudley, why didn't you say?'

The atmosphere in the room had changed. The fact that I was a writer of some importance was now of little or no consequence. All that was of consequence was the fact that Davie McVeigh had withheld something from Flora Cleverly.

'And have you turn the place upside down in preparation for a celebrity? I'm sure Miss Dudley would not have wished that. Am I right?'

He was gazing down at me once more, and in my embarrassment at the situation that I had unwittingly brought about I stammered, 'Yes – well, I mean, everything is quite all right as it is. The cottage is lovely—'

'There! Does that satisfy you?' Davie was looking once more towards Miss Cleverly. She had poured him out, I noticed, a cup of tea, but had not handed it to him. He now went behind the couch and took it from the side table; then he filled his plate with sandwiches before taking a seat in a chair to the right of Aunt Maggie near the empty fireplace from which, when he raised his eyes, he could look straight at me.

Roy McVeigh came and sat on the couch beside me. His opening remark did not alter my opinion that he was a nice young man, but it confirmed my suspicion that he was an ordinary one. 'I always wanted to write a book,' he said.

As he spoke, I heard my Aunt Maggie remark to Davie McVeigh in her conversational way, 'I see you go in for mushrooms.'

And the answer she received was, 'Oh, my God!'

But the older brother was not speaking to her. He was looking at his brother, and Roy, his face almost livid, was returning his scathing stare. But the incident was all over in a second.

Davie McVeigh had turned to Aunt Maggie and was saying, 'Yes, we go in for mushrooms, there's money in them; at least, there should be.' He paused before asking, 'Did you by any chance look into the cave yesterday when you came into the yard, Miss Fuller?' His tone was mildly inquisitive and quite civil, yet there was something behind it.

Aunt Maggie cast a quick glance in my direction before saying, 'Yes, yes, we did. We thought there might be someone inside who could guide us.'

'And you forgot to close the door?' David was smiling now.

It was I who answered him, and stiffly: 'No, we didn't forget to close the door. We purposely left it open because we found it open.'

His eyes were looking straight into mine. Then he said, 'Don't worry, I believe you.'

'Thank you!'

'You and that cave door – you dream about it half the time.' Miss Cleverly poured some water into the silver teapot.

'Oh, no, I don't, Flora. I'm not given to dreaming; there's no time. I only know that before I got into the car yesterday I saw to it that the door was closed, well closed, and, when I came back, it was open. I had let the stove go out.' He turned his head and addressed himself pointedly to Aunt Maggie now, looking sharply into her slightly perplexed countenance. 'If the weather had suddenly changed, say it had rained – if it had, it could have meant a drop in temperature. The matter of a few degrees applied often enough can ruin six months' work – not only that, it could ruin me.'

He gave a laugh – it was a pleasant sound – before adding, 'Never go in for mushrooms, Miss Fuller, unless you are very wealthy and can play at it as a hobby on a losing basis.'

I enquired of Roy McVeigh: 'Have you ever done any writing?' My motives for asking were mixed. I had resented Davie McVeigh's outrageous reaction to his brother's natural statement – natural, because writing a book is the desire of many people, and also I felt I must bring his attention from his brother at whom he was still staring. When I achieved this, he turned on me what could have been a glance of dislike, then drawing his lower lip in between his teeth he shook his head.

'No. No, I haven't,' he said, his voice sounding like that of a youth, a petulant youth.

'Don't you worry, Roy – if you want to write a book, you'll write a book. You can do anything you put your mind to.'

I looked over the back of the couch to Miss Cleverly, who was looking towards Roy McVeigh. Then she shifted her glance to me and added, 'Isn't that so, Miss Dudley?'

'Yes, yes. If you want to do a thing strongly enough, I am sure you can do it.'

I wasn't sure. I was just answering the woman the way she wanted to be answered. There was something here I couldn't understand. The tea party had turned into a battleground, but perhaps the battle had been raging before we had come into the house. I had the feeling that this was so – that it was a battle of long standing. Quite suddenly I found myself thinking, this woman loves one man and hates the other. And, from the little I had seen of the two men, I certainly couldn't blame her.

Even with stretching politeness to its limit, you could hardly say the tea was a pleasant interlude. I found it embarrassing, even unnerving, for the atmosphere from the moment Davie McVeigh had entered the room had been pervaded with bitterness.

A signal passed between Aunt Maggie and me which was achieved with our eyebrows, and I was about to rise to my feet when there came a tap on the open French window and all the occupants of the room turned towards it. The girl, Frannie, was standing there.

With an odd sort of stiff agility, I watched Davie McVeigh swing his heavy body up out of the low chair, but, before he was squarely on his feet, Miss Cleverly was at the window.

'Run along, Frannie, and play. That's a good girl.'

She was standing in front of the girl to prevent her entering the room.

'Leave her alone,' McVeigh's voice was quiet.

He did not thrust Flora Cleverly aside, but, in the position he took up, she was forced to step back into the room. He was now bending down towards the girl, talking softly in a different tone than any I had heard him use.

'Where have you been?' he asked. 'We haven't seen you for days . . . What's that?'

I could see him now holding up her arm and examining it. Then he looked at the other arm.

'Who did this?'

He was now touching Frannie's brow.

'Leave her alone. Her grannie's likely had to chastise her.' Flora Cleverly was seated once more, sipping at her tea now, and, addressing Aunt Maggie, she went on in a low tone. 'The girl gets out of hand – becomes very destructive. Her grannie has got to use the cane; it's the only way she can manage her.'

I prevented myself from saying, 'I don't believe it.' I wanted to rise and go towards the girl; however, I couldn't make myself do it when McVeigh was there. But now, although she was very reluctant to enter, he was drawing her into the room.

'I'll give that old girl a taste of her own medicine one of these days.' He was speaking as he pressed Frannie down on to the wooden seat near the fireplace.

'Not Grannie.'

'What! He looked down at her bent head. 'Who then?'

The girl shook her head and turned it away until she was staring into the empty fireplace.

'She'll get herself into trouble one of these days.'

So quickly did McVeigh swing round that I started nervously. He was glaring at Flora Cleverly and there was undisguised hate in his eyes but he did not speak.

In a way I admired the man for championing this poor undeveloped girl, but my condemnation of him was much greater than any approval I felt for his kindly attitude. For, no matter what he thought about his housekeeper, he had no right to treat her as he was doing in public. On the other hand, she had certainly goaded him more than a little.

When Frannie suddenly began to cry – and her

crying had a heart-rending sound – it had differing effects on us all. It brought a pitying look from Aunt Maggie. It brought Janie to kneel in front of her saying, 'Ah, Frannie, don't cry. Don't cry like that.' It made Flora Cleverly move quickly between the tables, pushing at the plates, arranging and rearranging their depleted contents. It brought Roy McVeigh's head drooping and his teeth pulling at his lips. The latter gesture I noted seemed to be characteristic of the young man. It drove Davie McVeigh onto the terrace outside the french windows. From there he called sharply, 'Frannie! Frannie, come here!'

The girl rose obediently, her head hanging, the tears dropping off her chin, and when she reached Davie McVeigh he held out his hand and she placed hers in it. I watched them walk over the lawn towards the road that rounded the hill and led to our cottage.

I was about to rise to my feet when Roy McVeigh spoke: 'Will you excuse me?' Getting up, he nodded towards Aunt Maggie before going hastily from the room, not through the french window, but out into the hall.

Flora Cleverly now came and took up her position on the home-made wool rug flanking the wide fireplace. She had her hands clasped loosely in front of her and her jaws moved back and forwards causing the wrinkles of her face to flow into each other before she spoke.

'I'm not going to apologize,' Flora said. 'You can't be expected to live on top of a family and not know all the ins and outs about them. We're no better or no worse than the next.'

'Oh, please don't apologize to us.' Aunt Maggie

was standing now, smoothing down the front of her dress.

'I'm not. I said I wasn't, and I'm not. I just made a statement. But you'll be able to pick out the gold from the dross for yourselves. It would be a very unusual family if it had all saints and no sinners, wouldn't it?' Flora was smiling at me as she put this question. But it was Aunt Maggie who answered her, saying, 'Very . . . very.'

'I made a pie this morning. I thought you would like it. If you'll just wait, I'll fetch it.'

If we had made any protest she would not have heard us, for in her lightning fashion she was out of the room so quickly it was impossible to realize she hadn't run or flown. And now we were left looking at each other, and Janie was looking at us, first at Aunt Maggie and then at me.

It was to me that Janie finally spoke, and what she said was, 'Davie's all right.'

Her tone was aggressive; it was as if she felt we were putting the blame for the whole scene on Davie McVeigh.

'He gets the backwash, always has.'

It was an odd, old expression to come from a child of ten, and it brought a twisted smile to Aunt Maggie's lips.

I was too embarrassed to answer and was relieved when Aunt Maggie asked, 'You are very fond of Mr McVeigh?'

'Yes, I am. And so was Doris.'

With this last statement, Janie cast a quick glance towards the hall door, then, with one more direct look shared between Aunt Maggie and myself, she turned and ran out of the french window. A moment later, Flora Cleverly came in with the pie which she handed to Aunt Maggie. I was glad, for I myself had a great desire to refuse her gift . . .

Aunt Maggie and I were walking back along the hill path towards the cottage but, so that she wouldn't be overheard, it wasn't until we were well past all the shrubbery and in the open that she began to talk.

'It would appear,' she said, 'that the lord of the manor has the loyalty of the young'uns at least.'

'And he would need it,' I said, 'for Flora Cleverly hates him.'

'They hate each other I would say. You know – ' Aunt Maggie turned her face towards me ' – it's a very queer set-up. If I were in your shoes I'd be saying to myself, here's the nucleus for a very good story.'

I smiled, then looked ahead. Perhaps my aunt was right, I thought. There was everything here for a story, certainly a background, one could even call it a 'romantic' background. I felt no pain at this moment as the world presented itself to me. The people in the house called Lowtherbeck were certainly heading for one big flare-up, and, unless I was very mistaken there was a deep underlying reason for it. But I couldn't compose a story without a love element of some sort, and there was no love element in that house so far as I could gather.

But wasn't I a writer? Couldn't I concoct such an element? If I did, it would be to bring it to an unhappy conclusion. And who would I make the hero, the one who fell in love, to be, in the end, frustrated? David McVeigh? – oh, no, not David McVeigh— And yet, why not? He had all the ingredients needed to make a lover, a strong, passionate, headstrong lover. I stopped dead on the hillside and looked down.

Aunt Maggie asked me, 'What is it?'

I just shook my head slowly before moving on again. In the shaking of my head, I was rejecting, clamping down heavily on the idea of the elder McVeigh as a hero of any story I would write. Roy, yes, perhaps, but David Bernard Michael McVeigh – never!

And no one had said a word of apology about last night – no one.

CHAPTER FOUR

When you have done something that surprises you, you search the past to see what elements precipitated your action. What surprised me was that I had now begun my novel and its hero was Davie McVeigh. This change of mind had come about through a series of incidents during the previous three weeks, but I think it really began on the hillside that Sunday afternoon. And it bore fruit one early dawn when I discovered what Davie McVeigh was hiding, but that was later.

On the Monday following that first Sunday at the cottage my aunt and I drove into the village of Borne Coote to replenish our supplies, or rather, stock up with tinned stuff and other necessities. And, as Borne Coote had only one actual shop, we were confronted for the second time with the little woman, Mrs Talbot, and, not only with Mrs Talbot, but Talbot himself. They were both behind the counter and they gave us the full benefit of their combined stares on our entrance. Then, with the embarrassing straightforwardness which seemed to be prevalent in this part of the country, the little woman, pointing at me, spoke.

'I thought you didn't know the McVeighs.'

'Nor did we when we were last here.' My reply was stiff.

'But you were going to the cottage – you were going to stay?'

'I made the arrangements through a Miss Cleverly. Does that explain things?' Aunt Maggie's head was cocked to one side.

'I told you so; I said it would be her that did all the arranging.'

Talbot was looking down at his wife. Then, turning his gaze towards Aunt Maggie, and seeming to pick up the tone of their last conversation, he said slowly, 'The misunderstanding is pardonable, madam. Now, what can I do for you ladies?'

Here was the businessman speaking.

We had written out an order and I handed it to him. The length of it seemed to please him, for he turned, and looking down on his wife, said, 'You leave this to me; get about your business.'

And Mrs Talbot got about her business. Talbot saw to us himself, going as far as to pack the goods in boxes and to place them in the boot of the car, assuring us as he did so that he would be pleased to be of service to us – any kind of service.

He explained, 'The shop's only me sideline, you see, ma'am.' (The 'ma'am' was divided between us now, it had taken the place of madam and miss.) 'I do a bit of taxiing, although there's not much in that line, except for a wedding and a late dance or such over in Penrith. An' I turn me hand to a bit of plumbing and decoratin'. Besides which, I'm the gravedigger for the three villages hereabouts. And in me spare time I go up and help Davie, big Davie. Now, there's a man for you.'

Talbot was pulling down the boot-lid of the car,

and he swivelled his long face towards me as he demanded, 'What do you think of big Davie?'

In case I might go so far as to forget myself and say what I did think of – big Davie, Aunt Maggie put in quickly, 'What do you do up there – at the house – Mr McVeigh's?'

'Oh, there's plenty to do up there. He'd have me full time if he could manage it. He thought he would be able to last year, but then he had to buy the horses.' He bent over Aunt Maggie and shook his long face in front of her as he stated: 'You can't grow mushrooms without manure, an' the cheapest way to have manure is to have horses, isn't it? Three he's got now, two old shires. The heavy ones are the best. Like old times to see horses on a farm, an' he uses them all, doesn't keep them just for—' He stopped, coughed, and added the information: 'Well, it's always better from working horses – they eat more, see? It's natural.'

I had got myself into the car. As on Saturday when these two had met, the desire to laugh rose in me. I dared not look at Aunt Maggie as she sat down beside me, but now Talbot's face was close to mine at the open window of the car.

'What do you think of Flora Cleverly?' This was asked in a loud whisper.

'What?'

'I asked, what do you think of her?'

'Well – er.' I glanced at Aunt Maggie, but Aunt Maggie was looking straight ahead. 'I should say she's a very capable housekeeper.'

'A very good featherer of nests if you ask me.' Talbot's nose was almost touching mine, and I couldn't get my head any further away from his long sombre face.

'You know she an' me nearly become related?'

'You did?'

'Aye, she was after me brother. He was gardener up there to the old people in the days when they had land to have gardens, if you know what I mean. But he upped an' skedaddled off to America.'

I shook my head.

'He died just three years gone. An' you know what?' He went on. 'Left her what he made.'

'Really?' I commented.

'Was it much?' This came from Aunt Maggie.

'Two thousand, seven hundred and fifty pounds. I contested it rightly but I lost 'cause we were only half-brothers really, and he had always fended for himself since he was a lad. Aye, Flora got the lot. But do you think she'll spend a penny on the place, or help Davie? No, not a brass farthin'. But she gives young Roy backhanders. Oh, aye, he's her bright boy is Roy, and the biggest cadger from here to—'

Talbot just managed to replace the destination with the name 'Cockermouth'. Then he continued. 'You be on guard, ma'am, if he comes askin' for a sub. You won't be the first one that Davie's had to refund money to afore they left.'

Again, I could only say, 'Really?'

'Aye, really.' The big nose was moving up and down now.

'Do you believe in jinxes?' Talbot asked now.

'Jinxes? – well, I don't know.'

'That means you don't believe in them, but there are such things. Davie's got a jinx on him; it's been put on him.'

Now Talbot withdrew his head a little from the window and his expression changed, even took on a semblance of hauteur. He said, 'I hope you ladies don't think I'm shootin' me mouth, but, as you're goin' to be up there for God knows how long, I thought it best to put you wise to a few things. Ladies are apt to get the wrong impressions at times – bit gullible like.'

And now he leaned forward again and almost across me, and addressed himself pointedly to Aunt Maggie this time. 'I'd like you to understand, ma'am, that I don't talk so glibly to everybody, but I'm concerned with them up at Lowtherbeck.'

'Yes, of course,' said Aunt Maggie.

Now that he thought Aunt Maggie understood the situation and the reason for his verbosity, Talbot withdrew himself, straightened up to his limit and inclined his head slowly downwards. And we took this as a signal that we now had his permission to depart.

We drove off and when we got into a quiet lane, we laughed – I laughed as I hadn't done for many months. Yet, in spite of our making kindly fun of him, I knew we had gathered more than groceries from Talbot's shop, and that we had met a man who could be a very good friend – to those he took to.

We did not return straight to the cottage, but did a round of sight-seeing going as far as Talbot's Cockermouth then on to Maryport, returning around Derwentwater and Keswick, past Ullswater, and on home. I thought of the cottage as home now.

It had been a long drive and, for the most part, a beautiful drive. When we arrived at the cottage about five o'clock, we were both rather tired; consequently,

I did not mount the stairs to put our things away until sometime after six. And it was as I opened the doors of the big cupboard that the sound came to me distinctly and brought my eyes upwards towards the ceiling. It was the sound of smothered weeping and I recognized it immediately.

Within a moment, I had mounted the ladder and pushed open the trap-door. There, on the floor, almost on eye-level with me, lay Frannie. She lifted her head when I entered and I was quick to note the look of disappointment coming into her eyes. Without getting from my hands and knees, I crawled the short distance to her, asking, 'What is it, my dear?'

On this, the girl turned her head from me and buried it once again in her arms.

'Don't cry like that, you'll make yourself ill. Come, sit up.' I put my hand on her shoulder, but, with the peevish attitude of a child, Frannie tried to shake it off.

'Come along.' I was coaxing her gently. 'Would you like a drink?'

There was no response.

'Come, don't cry like that – don't.'

The sound was hurting me. I wanted to take her in my arms and comfort her, and the next minute that's what happened – she was in my arms – brought there by the suggestion that I should take her over to the house.

'Come along, get up and I'll take you to the house,' I had said. On this, Frannie turned and flung herself on me, pressing her head between my breasts and gripping me with her arms as a frightened child clings to its mother.

'There now, there now. Don't – don't cry any more. What is it? Can't you tell me?'

It was at this point that Aunt Maggie's voice called up the stairs to me and I called back, 'Can you come up a minute?'

When I heard her come into the room down below my voice drew her to the foot of the ladder, and, twisting round on the floor, the girl still in my arms, I leant over the hole and said, 'It's Frannie; she's up here and upset about something. You'd better go and fetch one of them.'

At this, the girl's grip tightened about me and I looked down into Aunt Maggie's perplexed face and said quietly, 'Better try and find – him.'

Whether the girl knew to whom I referred I don't know, but she made no protesting movement.

I heard the creak of the stairs under Aunt Maggie's weight; then there was no sound except the girl's lessening sobs. She was lying now, her full weight on me, her head still pressed into my breasts, her arms gripping me, her legs entwined around mine, her whole attitude that of a child in distress. Stroking her hair, I looked around as I waited.

As McVeigh had said, there was plenty of bedding up here. Half of the small floor space seemed to be taken up with it. The rest of the floor, except where we were sitting, was covered with a conglomeration of books and soft stuffed animals, among them a panda and a teddy bear with long flopping ears. There were no dolls, I noticed. The only light came in through a minute skylight.

How long it was before I heard the quick scraping of footsteps on the stairs I don't know, but I had been aware for some time that one of my legs had gone to sleep and was now becoming very painful.

Davie McVeigh's head did not shoot into the attic, but rose slowly into the room, and he, too, did not rise to his feet but crawled forward.

Davie did not touch Frannie but asked gently, 'What is it?'

I had expected her to turn from me and fling herself on him, but she remained still.

'Frannie – Frannie, look at me.' Davie was bending down close to her now and his face was not more than inches from my own. His eyes were downcast and I noticed that the lids were heavy and fringed with short, thick, dark lashes. I felt embarrassed, slightly disturbed, and very uncomfortable as well. Trying to move my leg, I gave vent to a stifled groan. The lashes lifted and the eyes were looking into mine.

'I – I've got cramp.'

He bent forward to relieve me of Frannie and as his hand cupped her head his fingers touched the flesh of my neck near the breast. Instinctively, I recoiled. In a flash, his eyes were holding mine again.

His voice was low and cutting as he said, 'The action was involuntary.'

I wanted to say, 'I'm sorry.' But how could one explain a thing like that? What I did now was to try to loosen the girl's arms from around me, and, in doing this, I almost lost my balance and had to put my hands behind me to save us both from falling sideways. Then, with a movement that could only be called rough, Davie pulled Frannie from me and, gripping her by the shoulders, brought her round to face him.

Frannie did not protest. She was no longer crying but her head was hanging and she would not look at him.

'What is it? Tell me. Your grannie been at you?'

'No, Davie.'

'Someone said something to you?'

She shook her head.

'Have you been breaking things again?'

'No, Davie.'

He raised his eyes and looked at me. Then turning his gaze once more on Frannie, he smiled. It was a movement of his features I hadn't seen before. There was no sarcasm lifting the lips, no malice in the eye; his whole face looked gentle.

He said now, as he put his finger under the girl's chin, 'Come on, come on, you've got the hump. What do we say when we've got the hump?' He jerked her chin further up. 'Come on, what do we say?' he waited. Then he prompted slowly, 'Buck up and be a rabbit. Come on, say it.'

Frannie was looking at him now, her face unsmiling, but she repeated after him slowly: 'Buck up and be a rabbit.'

'Where's that book?' He was scrambling around the floor like a romping bear now. He pushed me aside slightly as he reached out and pulled towards him a large red-backed book. Then sitting down beside Frannie again, he said, 'Come on, we'll read some poetry – right out loud.' He pointed the words out with his finger and began:

Slowly Frannie repeated, 'Promise to look at a leaf on a tree.'
Then she went on in halting fashion:

'Promise to look at a leaf on a tree,
Promise me, promise me;
Promise to stand and look at the sea—'

Then breaking off, she turned her eyes up to his and tears were in them once more as she whimpered, 'I can't, Davie, I can't.'
Gently Davie laid the book down by his side – which was almost against my knee – and cupping Frannie's face with his thick square hands he asked in a perplexed fashion, 'What is it, Frannie? You can tell me. Someone has frightened you. Tell me – who?'
I watched her look at him for a moment, then lower her head, and after she lowered it, she shook it from side to side.
'You'd better tell me – ' his voice was softly insistent ' – because I'll find out anyway. I find out everything, don't I?'
At this, like a slowly overbalancing sack, Frannie drooped forward and lay against him, her head buried in his open coat.
Over the top of her head, he looked at me and asked, 'How long has she been here?'
'I don't know. We've been out all day.'
'Come on. We're going home.'
He made a movement to rise to his feet, but, as he did so, the girl pressed herself tighter to him.
He said sharply, 'Now, Frannie! No more of it. I'm taking you home.'

Then, very much with the reaction of a father who had stood enough from a petulant child, he put his arm around her middle and drew her towards the ladder. Holding her like a bundle of bedding, he descended into the bedroom and placed her on her feet.

He turned and, looking up at me, asked brusquely, 'You coming down?'

'I'll manage, thank you.'

'Good enough.'

I sat on the floor where he had left me, the red-backed book in my hand. Frannie was an odd creature but so, indeed, was he. 'Promise to look at a leaf on a tree'. I looked down at the book. It was a loose-paged book comprised of thick handmade paper, and on each page, in spidery italic writing, was a verse of some kind – I would not have called it poetry. The book had a frontispiece which bore the date, January 24th, 1919, which was followed by the strange inscription: 'Came home today with the desire to live.'

Further down the first page, standing alone, were the words: Buck up and be a rabbit. On the opposite page were two verses – the words which Davie McVeigh had tried to get the child to repeat. I read them slowly:

Promise to look at a leaf on a tree,
  Promise me, promise me.
Promise to stand and look out to sea,
  Promise me, promise me.
And at noon on the day look up to the sky,
And make it a habit. Try, Try.

But if you haven't a tree, or the sea, or sight,
What will you promise me?
To reach inside and find the spark
That started the tree, gave sight, and the sea, and so say with me:
Buck up and be a rabbit.

The sentiment was simple, but charming. I turned over the pages. The book was full of such pieces, simple rhymed philosophy. I wondered who had written it. There was no name on the book, but the date was 1919. Likely, McVeigh's father – very likely.

Besides the litter of books on the floor, I saw tucked neatly in the corner, a pile of books dealing principally with art, bearing such titles as *Perspective* and *The Art of Etching* by Rex Vicat Cole. There were books on woodwork and large flat books that spoke of art plates. But what drew my attention at once was a piece of paper hung between two stacks of books on which was written simply: 'Don't touch.'

The command I felt was meant for Frannie and not for the tenants of the cottage. It gave me a strange insight into the relationship between these two people. Davie McVeigh had placed that order there knowing that, although the girl would be alone in the attic, she would obey it.

My Aunt Maggie called again from the kitchen, and I descended into the bedroom and then to the ground floor, to be greeted by Aunt Maggie not with: 'What was she upset about?' but with 'I don't like that woman!'

'Miss Cleverly?'

'The same.'

Aunt Maggie turned and marched into the sitting-room, and I followed her. And sitting down there, she looked up at me and said, 'I nearly broke my neck getting there. It was her I saw first; she was in a confab with the younger one, Roy. Those two are as thick as thieves. I must have surprised her when I called through the kitchen window, for she turned on me. You wouldn't believe it but her face was really contorted with fury. The young fellow was sitting at the kitchen table and she had her arm around his shoulders. When I had called, they had both been startled – and she actually yelled at me. "What are you doing there?" she asked. And, when I told her – she was at the door by now and slightly calmer – she said, "Oh, that girl is becoming a proper nuisance. I'll have to tell her grannie to keep her home. You'd better go and see what's up with her, Roy."' After a pause: 'You know something, Pru?'

I shook my head negatively.

'There's something between those two. He calls her "Aunt Flora". "I can't do that, Aunt Flora," he said. "I'm due back – I'm taking over for Fenwick. I told you." Did you know that the young one was only a garage hand?'

'No, I didn't know what he was.'

'Well, the way she put it was, he was in the car business and they were very busy at the present moment. But, by the look of his overalls, he had been under a number of cars. It's odd, don't you think, that he hasn't been put to something different from a car mechanic?'

'There's money in cars today, Aunt Maggie.'

'Yes, there might be in the big garages, but I shouldn't imagine there's much in that line in the garages around these quarters.'

'It may be a garage on the main road.'

'Perhaps. Anyway, she told me to go to the shed – that's what she called that cave – she pointed across to it. She said I would find McVeigh in there and to tell him. And do you know something else?'

Again I shook my hand.

'When I walked in, he nearly hit the roof. He was laying pipes or such from that coke stove, and when I pushed the door open I must have moved them out of line. Anyway, he calmed down when he saw it was me and not you.' Aunt Maggie grinned at me. 'And he was off like a shot when I told him about the girl.'

Now Aunt Maggie screwed her eyes up, and nodding her head at me, she ended: 'You know, Pru, I don't like this set-up at all, and, the less we have to do with the folks in that house, the more comfortable will be our stay.. At least, that's how I see it. How do you feel?'

'I don't really know,' I said. 'I'm only sure of one thing – and that is that David McVeigh is more objectionable than any of the others.'

Later that night, the weather broke with a really terrifying storm. There was a thunderclap that drove Aunt Maggie and me to cling together. We had been watching the lightning streaking over the hill beyond the lake, and one flash seemed to stab the lake right in its centre. Following that, the thunder-clouds burst above us.

We went to bed early, voting it the best place to be as we were cold. I would have lit a fire if there had been anything with which to light one. I guessed that the main fuel used was wood, and, although there was evidence of logs having been stacked against the back wall, at present there were not even any chips there with which to make a flame.

So it was early the next morning, while it was still raining, that I made my way over to the house to see about some form of heating. I made the trip reluctantly, I fear, and would gladly have left it to Aunt Maggie. Surprisingly, she had expressed a preference to stay in bed that morning, as she felt as if she had a slight cold coming on. I knew this was a sensible decision, for the room downstairs, although attractive in the sunlight, was fireless and, lacking any form of heating, it had lost something of its charm. So, as I said, I went to the house.

Thinking I would encounter someone in the courtyard, I went straight there, but there was no one to be seen. So I crossed over towards the kitchen, but at the sound of Miss Cleverly's voice, I stopped before I reached the door or the kitchen window.

Miss Cleverly was saying, 'How do I know why he's decided to sell the land? You should have been here instead of in your bolt hole.'

There came a pause. Then I actually heard a deep intake of breath before the deep, guttural voice of Davie McVeigh ground out his answer.

'Flora Cleverly,' Davie was saying, 'you'll try me too far one of these days and I'll throw you out on your neck. I warn you, mind, I'll do it, because you've stripped me of all sentiment concerning you or anything you've done in the past.'

'Oh, be quiet! Don't act the big fellow with me. You'd be finished flat if I left here, and you know it. Who'd work like I have done for years for nothing? And supplied the food for many a mouth at that? You can't do without me, and you know it. Everything you touch dies on you.'

'Yes, because you've willed it. Don't think I don't know who left that shed door open. That's the third time it's happened since I spawned the beds.'

'I've told you I didn't touch the shed door; it was them two up at the cottage nosing about.'

'I'd believe them before I'd believe you, Flora. But that's beside the point. What I want to know is, what made Alec Bradley decide to sell that bit of land and the cottage? The old woman has lived there since she was a child. What's going to happen to her and to Frannie?'

'Don't ask me. I don't know. If you make them your concern, that's up to you – and while I'm on about it, whose concern is it? It's puzzled me a bit why you should trouble yourself so much about the pair of them. It wouldn't have been you who was after her mother, would it? Funny, if I'm hitting the nail on the head.'

There came a long silence, during which I found myself backing cautiously away. It wasn't until I reached the beginning of the courtyard again that I heard McVeigh's voice and the end of his reply as he came bursting out of the door.

He was shouting: 'It's a wonder you weren't hit on the head a long time ago.'

I almost ran round to the front of the house and I was about to mount the steps to ring the bell when I heard the clink of heavy boots coming in my direction on the stones of the courtyard. So, as if having just made my appearance, I walked back towards the end of the house, and there came up with Davie McVeigh.

I have said earlier that the man's complexion was a ruddy brown, but I now saw that it was grey. His cheeks seemed to have been pulled in and he looked much older at this moment than I had yet seen him. Although he looked straight at me, I am positively sure he did not see me. When I spoke, as I did rapidly out of embarrassment, he jerked his head a little to the side before bringing his eyes back to focus on my face.

' – and my aunt's in bed with a slight cold and we would like a fire – if that is possible,' I finished.

'A fire? Yes. Oh, yes. Of course.'

Again, he shook his head. Then, to my astonishment, he began to apologize. 'I'm sorry about this. Of course, you need a fire. I generally see to a load of wood being dumped before anyone goes in – summer or winter. It's always cool in the evening.' He, too, was talking rapidly now. 'I'll get Talbot to saw some up – he should be along shortly. But in – ' he turned from me ' – in the meantime, you'd better have an oil heater.'

So unexpectedly civil had he been, so unlike himself, that I answered, 'I'm sorry that I have put you to all this trouble.'

I was following him back across the yard in the direction of the cave wall now, and, as he looked at me over his shoulder, I fully expected some remark, such as, 'And so am I.'

But what Davie said was: 'We've slipped up a lot where you and your aunt are concerned – the place wasn't ready and it should have been. But I suppose you can lay that down to the wedding.' As he pushed open the door and stood aside to allow me to enter, he added, 'They don't happen every day, do they?'

My back was stiffening again. Was he probing? If he had known who I was he had likely got his information from the splash the papers made about the court case and the break-up of my marriage.

We were in the cave now, all the way in, and, for a moment, my mind was diverted from him by what I saw. Stretching away into the far distance was what looked like an allotment, and covering the surface was a network of grey stuff, like solidified mist.

'The – the beginning of the mushrooms?' I pointed.

'Yes. This is the spawn. It's doing fine. It's all ready for the casing now – that is, the soil that goes on top.'

'It's very interesting. Can you make a living out of them – a reasonable living?'

I wasn't really interested in the mushrooms, nor yet in whether McVeigh would be able to make a living from them, not at this moment – for I was almost overcome with the oppressive atmosphere of the place.

'Yes. Yes, I can make a living, if I get the chance.'

On his last words, his head went down and he turned away and walked along the path bordering the beds. I could do nothing but follow him. There had been some light given off by a weak electric bulb, but now, walking away from it, I could barely make out his back in front of me, until he came to a stop in front of the cave wall. There, in the Open-Sesame manner, he pushed at what must have been a door, and we passed into another cave, which was cooler and much lighter. After a moment, I saw that this cave got its light and air from two sources – from an open door in the far distance and from a sort of funnel in the rock that opened up just above my head.

I was looking upwards, trying not to gulp openly at the refreshing air, when Davie said, 'I'm going to do something with that when I get round to it. The wind whistling down there in the winter would cut you in two, and that's no use for mushrooms. That's why one's got to be so careful about doors.'

Our glances crossed for a brief second on this last remark but I did not take it up. Instead, I said, 'It's an amazing size. You'd never dream from outside that there was so much space in here.'

'It's wasted.' Davie flung his hand out with an impatient movement. 'I use it as a storeroom, but one day—' He nodded his head – he seemed to have made a promise to himself.

We were moving towards the far doorway now. Again addressing his back, I asked, 'How does one start a business like this?' For the moment I had forgotten that I didn't like the man; I suppose it was my writer's instinct at work gathering data.

'You go to school and learn.'

'School?' The word was high in my head.

He had stopped and was looking at me. 'Well, sort

of. When you want to get mushrooms beyond a backyard and a seed-box business, you've got to learn many things. There's much more in it than people think. But, whichever way you do it, there's the secret.' He had stepped through the doorway and was pointing across a wide farmyard to an open barn beyond, within which was a great mound of steaming manure. 'Preparation of that,' he said. 'But it becomes so damned scientific, I sometimes wonder how the mushrooms managed before the lads started on them. That's the worst part. You turn that stuff until you hate the sight of it.'

'Have you been growing them long?'

'Three years. But I was nearly finished last year – the crop went dead on me. There can be two a year, you know – if you're lucky. But, when a thing like that happens, it can knock you back somewhat.'

'Yes, yes.'

Our glances had crossed again, and I looked away from him at the farmyard. I saw that it was bordered on one side by stables, on another by byres. In a field beyond the open barn, were a number of small black hutches which I knew to be chicken runs.

I turned to him, and, my voice showing my genuine amazement, I said, 'You would never dream that this lay behind the caves – I mean the hill – not from the other side – the courtyard side.'

'No. It is rather surprising.'

I looked up at the wall of the stone-cased hill. 'It's like a basin,' I said. 'It looks much bigger inside than it does out.'

'It is. This hill gives no indication whatever of the size of the caves inside. They go for miles. I haven't even been in some myself – too big to get through the passages.'

'Really?' I was finding my interest deepening. 'How were they discovered?'

'Discovered? Oh, they've always been there, as far as I understand. My great-grandfather used to hide whisky in the far ones when they used to distil the stuff in the hills around here and were on the run from the Excise. They used to search the caves, but more often than not they got lost themselves and had to be brought out – now, there's material for a story.'

He was actually smiling at me in a kindly fashion. He didn't seem the same person whom I'd heard talking to Flora Cleverly not more than minutes ago. He not only looked agreeable, he sounded agreeable. I had the fanciful thought that passing through the caves had cleansed him of his roughness, brusqueness, and boorish manner.

David McVeigh stood now rubbing his hand over the head of a collie dog which was pressed close to his knee. Near a gate at the far end of the yard, with their heads well over it, stood two heavy feathery-footed horses – Talbot's shires.

It had stopped raining. There was no sun, yet this place seemed lit up in a fashion I couldn't describe. I sensed it. And I felt accurately that it was in this part of Lowtherbeck, and only in this part, that this man could feel at ease. I could see him, as it were, cut off from the rest of the household, working here and sleeping at the cottage. He need hardly come in touch with anyone at the house unless he wanted to – I cut off my thinking about him abruptly. I did not want to have to change my opinion of him.

I asked now, 'Do you have help?'

'Only occasionally. Talbot, you know, from the village, when he can give me a few hours. But Janie is a grand help; she's got a marvellous way with the animals. But from today, she's back at school. Her sister Doris – that's the one who was married on Saturday – she was very handy, too. And there's Roy; he helps when he can. We get by.' He squared his shoulders. 'It all gets done in the end.' Again, it seemed as if he was assuring himself instead of making a statement.

I knew absolutely nothing about farming and the work it entailed, yet I would have had to be a very stupid person if I hadn't realized that there was a great deal too much work here for one man with occasional help to get through.

As if reading my thoughts, Davie said, 'There's a bit overmuch for one, yet not enough for two.'

'Your brother works away?'

'Yes, he's in the car business. And that's what he likes – he can't stick this.' He moved his arm to indicate the yard. Then, as if he had been betrayed into saying too much, he added abruptly, 'I'll get you a stove and oil.'

When he came out of a shed carrying a stove and a can of oil, I said, 'I can manage these. I'll make two journeys.'

'No. It won't take me but a few minutes to go there and back. Come this way.'

I could see he would brook no argument and I did not protest, but again followed him. Once more I experienced surprise for, as he said, it was only a matter of minutes before I saw the cottage – but the back of it this time. He had brought me through a narrow overgrown path that I guessed had been used before only by himself. It came out in the thicket behind the sentry-box lavatory. Another minute, and we were in the sitting-room. He did not simply deposit the things, but he filled the stove and lit it.

'There,' he said as he looked at the stove after it had given a final *plop plop*, and settled down to glow. 'That should be all right now. And I'll see you have the wood this afternoon. By the way—'

He had turned from me and was walking towards the kitchen as he spoke. His walk was slow, his head was bent downwards, and his words seemed muffled as he said, 'I wonder if you would mind Frannie coming to the attic occasionally? It's the only place she can feel – well – ' I thought he was going to say 'safe', and I'm sure he was, but he changed it to: ' – at home. She's played up there since she was a small girl. She gets fits of moodiness and likes to be by herself.'

I hesitated in my reply because my mind had jumped back to the conversation I had heard from the courtyard concerning the child and her grandmother.

Davie turned to me and said, 'I'm sorry. I shouldn't have asked.'

I stammered, 'Oh really, please, it's perfectly all right. Yes, tell her to come when she likes. She won't be in our way.'

'You are sure?'

'Yes, perfectly.'

I wasn't perfectly sure. If I had stopped to think

and told myself the truth, I didn't want anyone coming in and out of the cottage, least of all this lost soul of a girl, for I found she disturbed me emotionally, and I myself was staying here to calm my own emotions.

'Thanks.'

David McVeigh was standing outside the back door and, before turning abruptly and striding away, he said – in a tone that was an echo of what I had come to look upon as his natural disgruntled voice – 'If you want anything just tell me.'

As he did not wait for my reply, I did not offer any, but returned to the room, thinking of the words of Flora Cleverly: 'If you make them your concern, that's up to you – and while I'm on about it, whose concern is it? It's puzzled me a bit why you should trouble yourself so much about the pair of them. It wouldn't have been you who was after her mother, would it? Funny, if I'm hitting the nail on the head.'

CHAPTER FIVE

We had been in the cottage, as I have said, for over three weeks now, and I was feeling much better. I had had no bout of nerves, no trembling, no retching, and no fear. That indescribable panicky fear and inability to describe what I was afraid of had not returned.

And during this time, I had, in a way, come to know quite a lot about the occupants of Lowtherbeck. I learned, for instance, that Flora Cleverly had actually been born in the cottage. Her father had been a sort of working manager of the estate. She had been brought up side by side with Davie McVeigh's father, John McVeigh, and she had helped in the big house long before John McVeigh had married.

I further learned, from short conversations I had had with Roy, that, compared to his brother, he was of rather low if not exactly dim intellect, and the rude exclamation that Davie McVeigh had made when Roy had said he had always wanted to write a book was now understandable to me, although I still thought the remark had been unnecessary. As for Janie, I found her a nice child, but I saw little of her. Likely, she spent all her time helping with the animals as McVeigh had said.

Then McVeigh himself. Had he kept up his pleasant manner towards me? Yes – yes – strangely enough, yes. I had been amazed at his change of front, yet I had had further proof that under this thin skin of civility still lay the demanding, dogmatic master of all he surveyed. This was proved one morning when I came upon him and the man Alec Bradley in the farmyard behind the hill. It was almost a week from the time that he had brought me through the caves and shown me the short cut to the cottage. From then on, I had used that way when going for the milk. I was just about to come out of the overgrown pathway one morning when I heard Davie McVeigh's voice raised high in anger.

Davie was saying, 'The hell you will! Not if I can stop you. There's something behind this.'

'There's nothing behind this except that I want to plough my own land.'

I would not have recognized Alec Bradley's voice from my memory of it on the night of the mad dance near the lake, but, from where I stood, I could see his profile with his chin thrust out. It was the same man who had shouted out the rhyme.

'You can't plough within twenty yards of the cottage – it's solid rock underneath. If you want to plough, plough round it and leave a path to the road.'

'I'm pulling it down.'

'By God! I'll see you don't!'

'Try and stop me.'

'Aye, I'll stop you. You take my word for it, Bradley. I'll stop you. I've still got some say around here.'

'Pooh! Don't try to bluff me. Everything you've touched has dropped to pieces under your hand for years. You're nothing but a byword. An' I'm warning you, I'm not drunk this time, so don't try anything with your fists. But you won't, will you, because Cissie's in the car above on the road watching us. You wouldn't like Cissie to see you hit out first, would you? You've never been the same since you lost Cissie to me – and then to go and lose young Doris to Jimmy. It was another bad blow, wasn't it?'

'Get out!'

'I'm goin', but I just stepped in to warn you. Keep your nose out of affairs that don't concern you. Even Meg Amble herself doesn't want you interfering. She's all set to go down to her brother in Dorset, an' the girl with her.'

'You're a liar!'

'Go and ask her!'

'Get out!'

I waited a while until I heard the car on the road beyond start up. Then I still waited – for Davie McVeigh had not moved from the spot on which he had stood while talking to Alec Bradley, and something in the look on his face warned me not to make my presence known, yet for some unexplainable reason I wanted to go to him. I was just about to turn round and go back to the cottage when I saw him stride over to what was presumably a chopping block and there, lifting up the axe high, he swung it down and buried its head in the scarred wood.

The action was so ferocious, so terrifying, that I found my breath checked by my own hand pressed tightly across my mouth. The next thing, I had turned without taking heed to be quiet and was running along the narrow path to the cottage; and I didn't stop running until I was actually in the sitting-room.

Aunt Maggie, who had been sitting before the fire,

turned startled eyes on me. And then, rising quickly, she asked anxiously, 'What is it? What's happened?'

'Nothing. Nothing.' I shook my head. Then going towards the burning logs, I held my hands out to the blaze.

'You're shivering.' Her hand was on my arm. 'What is it? Something's happened.'

'Not to me. Don't worry. It was—' I sat down on the couch, then told her of the scene I had just witnessed, and ended, 'It was the fury with which he wielded that axe, as if he were hitting out at the man, this Alec Bradley. And not only him.' I shook my head and closed my eyes tightly. 'I just don't know; I've never seen anyone so angry before.' For a fleeting moment, I remembered my own anger against the man who had deceived me, but it was not comparable with the anger of Davie McVeigh. His anger seemed to be against the whole world – except, perhaps, the girl Frannie, and young Janie.

Aunt Maggie was looking straight into the fire now. She had her hands joined on top of her knees and her body was rocking gently back and forth. This movement indicated that she was troubled.

I said quickly to her, 'Don't worry; *I'm* not upset. It's odd, but – I was frightened, and yet I wasn't – I can't explain. I had to run away – because if I hadn't, I would have run forward to him, and I felt I mustn't.' My voice trailed off.

Aunt Maggie had turned her head and was looking at me. She said quietly, 'Look, lass, things are not turning out the way I thought. What about us making a move, eh? We can even pay them the full amount. They seem hard up, the lot of them. What about it, eh?'

I considered for a moment. Yes, we could easily pay them the remainder of the three-months rent and pack and leave this moment – we had nothing but clothes with us. But, wherever we stayed this night, I knew that I would be thinking back to this cottage and what was happening to Davie McVeigh and those concerned with him.

It was I who was looking into the fire now, and I spoke slowly as if reading my own thoughts: 'The doctors said I had to fight this thing – didn't they – this thing that has urged me for years to give up and let life walk past me. This thing that won't even let me finish with life. They said that, if I wanted to win the battle, I had to do exactly the opposite. I had to take an interest in things outside myself – pretend an interest, even if I didn't feel it, and, eventually, the shadow life would take on some form of reality. Well, Aunt Maggie, as you know, I've been trying hard for many months with little result, yet here in this out-of-the-way place I think the shadow is turning into reality because I've become interested in the people in that house in an odd way.' I looked at her now. 'I can't explain it except to say that I suppose it's the writer in me coming alive again. But I want to keep going there and finding out things. I'm not being nosy, you know that.'

Aunt Maggie's hand was patting mine now and she smiled as she said, 'That's good news anyway, and if the place and that lot are having such a heartening effect on you we'll take it on a three-year lease—'

Between that morning and the time I want to describe now, I only met Davie McVeigh three times. I had seen him in the distance, but, even at the distance of a few yards, he took no notice of me, seeming unaware of my presence. But at the other times when he did speak to me, his manner and tone were back to what I thought of as the 'real' David Bernard Michael McVeigh. And then came the morning of the soft dawn, the morning when I knew I had a story, when I knew I had a story of the house, of Lowtherbeck and the people therein.

I had been restless all evening and took my restlessness to bed with me. This was often the case when a story was brewing in my mind. I dropped into fitful sleep and woke as the light was just breaking over the lake, revealing the mist as a grey net that was being dragged gently across the water. I opened the window further and leant out. The air was cool but not cold. It was going to be a lovely day, a rare September day.

Previously, when I had woken up at this time of the morning and had not had this view to look upon, my mind had turned inwardly to my own troubles and coated them further with resentment, but, since I had slept on this narrow bed with my head on a level with this window, my thoughts had been drawn outwards, as my whole being was being drawn outwards at this moment. I wanted to walk near the lake.

I strained my eyes towards the travelling clock. It said half-past five. If I were to get up now, I would likely disturb Aunt Maggie. But the urge to get outside conquered consideration for my aunt. I was wearing a short nightie, but did not take it off; I just pulled a skirt and twin-set sweater over it. Then, donning my slippers, I crept quietly towards and down the stairs. In the kitchen, I changed my footwear, and going from the room, I opened the door.

The daylight was creeping higher into the sky now. It seemed to be drawing night shrouds from the trees, trailing them like stencilled veils over the dewy, weeping grass. Slowly, like one entranced, I walked down to the lake. But here the picture had changed. I couldn't see the edge of the water – I couldn't see my feet either. I was now walking in a swirl of mist. It was a slightly eerie, yet wonderful, feeling. The hill beyond the lake was showing a pale mauve tint; it looked high and far away like a mountain and of a sudden I had the desire to climb it. I had walked round the foot of it a number of times. The hill rose from a valley bottom which was a field with a boundary wire running down its middle. I had never been to the top, and now I was going to climb it.

As I walked in the mist-covered grass, I experienced a feeling that was not joy. I knew what joy felt like – this was not joy. Was it contentment? No. No. There was nothing static about it. In fact, one of its ingredients was a desire to run, to skip like a child over the carpeted ground.

At one period I lifted my feet high in a dancing step almost, then admonished myself, 'Don't be silly!' Nerves didn't always show themselves in despondency; they often took the form of high laughter, and silly antics – one must be aware. I found myself shaking my head to throw off my own admonition. I was always too careful, always watching myself. Suddenly, I heard the voice in my head saying, 'Run if you want to; go on,' and I obeyed. I ran through the mist until I reached the foot of the hill, and then I began to climb, and, as I climbed the sun climbed with me. When, panting and laughing to myself, I reached the top, I stood in its light and it warmed me through to my heart.

I had not felt like this for years; truthfully, I had never felt like this in my life before. I knew in this moment I was beginning to live and was experiencing life as I had never done. I knew also that, whatever happened to me in the future, I myself would be in the forefront of its creation. The misfortunes which had happened to me in the past had come through my mother and father – and through Ian. I felt now, and with deep conviction, that not one of the three could touch me again . . .

Why don't such moments last? Perhaps they are just given to us to use as a memory of strength with which to combat our fear when it descends on us again. Perhaps this moment I was experiencing was what is meant by drawing strength from nature. Anyway, I had the urge to throw my arms wide, so forceful was this feeling of new life within me, but warned myself that I was on a high elevation and could be seen. Yet, who would be about at this time of the morning? Who, except myself? I had the world to myself. It was as I gazed over this world that I caught a glimpse of the Big Water.

I had never been near the Big Water and when I blinked the sun from my eyes and shaded my vision, I could see part of it quite clearly. Away across an open stretch of land, which headed the top of the Lil Water – which I could just make out from my bedroom window – was a deep belt of trees. This was the border of the Big Water.

I was going towards the border now. I was going

to see the Big Water. I was running down the hill. There was no mist here; that is, until I reached the valley, when once again it swirled round my ankles.

Before I could cross the open land, I had a barrier to surmount. It was a dry-stone wall; many of them intersected the fields in these parts. But this one was about four feet high and two feet thick and its top was rough and hurt my hands and knees. Although I was now in the valley, the land was still on a slope, and, as I gripped the top of the stonework to heave myself over, I had a momentary impression of men struggling with these great boulders, carrying them up the incline, lifting them into place – all without the help of machinery. These were the men from the stock who had fought to defend this country against the Scots. No wonder they gloried in being tough.

I was not thinking so much of Davie McVeigh at this moment as of Talbot, and was remembering the day he brought the wood to the cottage. He had taken up a great pile of logs in his arms and brought them into the sitting-room; I had remarked about their being too heavy to carry at one go. Talbot had turned on me a look that was almost scornful. Then, over a cup of coffee in the kitchen, he had regaled me with stories of the ghosts of Cumberland and the achievements of her men. It was only when he started to relate the passionate romances of some of the ladies of the county that I withdrew. There were still certain subjects I could not listen to, and one of them was the romantic loves of others.

But this memory fled, wiped away by the floating mist. I was over the wall now. I found I had to tread carefully, because twice I almost stumbled, for the field was undoubtedly studded with small outcrops of rock.

Then, as if it had been pushed aside by a giant hand, the mist drifted away as I entered the trees. When I emerged on the other side, there was nothing before me but a large stretch of water – at least four times the size of the cottage lake.

I was disappointed in the setting. It did not have the attractiveness of the Lil Water. Although it was bordered for quite some way by trees and had the advantage of what looked, from this distance, like a miniature beach, there was something forbidding about the entire scene. There was a rowboat lying on its side away to the right. It was old and unused and I wondered if it were the same boat that had capsized and drowned Frannie's parents.

Although the morning sun was touching the water, it did not seem to add any warmth to it. I was reluctant to go farther. I said to myself: 'Don't be silly. Walk around it; it's only a lake.' But, instead of doing so, I sat down on a low flat-topped boulder near the fringe of the trees. It was as if the excitement of the morning were seeping out of me. I felt rather tired and I recognized, with a feeling of dread, that a depression was descending upon me. I looked around. I was very susceptible to atmosphere – I had found this out long ago. Perhaps I was experiencing this feeling because two people had died in this water. And not only two – there could have been many victims down the generations who had started to cross this lake and never reached the other side. Yet why should it affect me so adversely? I didn't know.

I was about to make the effort to rise and retrace

my steps when there came a movement in the trees away to my right. It brought my head round and then my mouth open as I saw – walking down the miniature beach – Davie McVeigh. I saw him drop something from his hand – it could have been a coat. I realized that he was naked, but what brought my hand up to my face was the fact that my eyes were conveying to my senses a horror because I was not looking at naked flesh, but at limbs that were covered in patches with a sickly looking light pink skin, and in between the patches were patterns formed by scarred flesh – in some places, it was drawn together in a series of weals. The weals moved as his muscles worked; they rippled like dissected snakes with each step he took. I found myself repeating Aunt Maggie's reverent phrase: 'My God!' I said to myself. Then I added, 'Oh, dear God!'

This, then, was why Davie always wore his shirt buttoned up to the neck and the cuffs of his sleeves fastened. But when his body was scarred like this, how had his face escaped? I had noticed a broad scar leading from his collar to the back of his ear and thought it might have been the result of a war wound. A great many men carried these badges of war on them, but he was surely too young to be carrying such a badge. Nevertheless, this man was carrying more than a badge, he was carrying a burnt body around with him. I found myself standing on my feet, my head shaking slowly. I was thinking: what does one know of another? I detested this man – at least, I had detested him. I looked upon him as a sneering, arrogant individual, yet all the time he was carrying, behind the façade of the big he-man, this scarred body.

One thing only was important now – I must get away quietly – he mustn't see me. Knowing I had seen him exposed would be unbearable for him.

Forgetting that I had risen from the stone and it was now behind me, I took a step backwards; then, unable to save myself, I toppled over, twisting as I did so and landing on my side. There was a pain in my elbow and wrist, for my arm had been thrust out to break my fall, but I leaned on it now and I turned my head slowly and looked to where Davie McVeigh was standing facing me. The same distance was between us as before, yet he seemed to be almost breathing down on me. After a brief glance at him, I lowered my head. The front of his body bore the same pattern as the back.

From under my eyelids, I watched his feet moving, not towards me but towards the belt of trees again. His feet weren't hurrying; their pace was steady. I made an effort to rise, but when I put pressure on my hand the pain was agonizing, and I found myself stretched on my side again. After a moment, I sat up with the aid of my other hand and rested my back against the boulder, gripping my hurt wrist the while. I made no effort to get up and hurry away. I was waiting – the next move would be his. It was only two or three minutes later that I saw him walking towards me with his coat on. I did not look at him when he approached. When he came to a stop, I still did not raise my eyes to his.

'Well!'

The word had a tight sound yet did not give any indication of anger.

I glanced up and found myself stammering. 'I – I came out to see the dawn. I didn't mean—'

'You needn't apologize. I remember you telling me once before that it's a free country. And take that frightened look off your face.'

'I'm – I'm not frightened.'

'You're frightened all the time. Aren't we all?' He turned his face away from mine now and looked over the water. I was surprised at the momentary feeling of resentment that filled me, swamping my pity for the man – resentment that once again he was, as it were, taking the wind out of my sails. I had expected him to rage at me and, in my compassion for him, I had been willing to submit to his rage without rising against it. But here he was turning the tables.

McVeigh was still looking at the lake as he said, 'You are frightened. Oh – ' he shook his head slowly ' – not of me. You pride yourself that you can see through me, don't you? No, you're not afraid of me, but you're afraid of everything else – don't get up.' He turned and held the palm of his hand towards me. Then he added, 'I can sit down; I've got at least half an hour before the day starts. Have you hurt your hand?'

McVeigh was sitting not more than a foot from me, his legs stretched out from under his coat, his bare feet pointing upwards. I found I was looking at them. There was no contorted skin on them – the skin was natural and the feet were broad and well-shaped.

I said, 'I think I've sprained my wrist.'

'Let's see.'

I did not extend my hand towards him, and, when his fingers touched my wrist, the reaction was the immediate stiffening of my muscles, mostly in the region of my stomach.

He felt this tenseness, I knew, for his fingers remained stationary for a moment and his hard gaze brought my eyes to him. There we sat for some seconds looking at each other. Then he asked quietly, 'What's made you like this? You should never let anything get on top of you to this extent. You should fight it.'

To my amazement, I heard myself saying quietly, 'I am fighting it.'

'Was it because of the break-up?' The muscles were more tense now and I was unable to answer, so he went on quietly, as his fingers moved over the bones of my hands.

'These things happen, they happen to us all – in different ways. The world of people and incidents beats you up, kicks you around, and you've only got one life to answer with.'

His fingers released my wrist as he said, 'There's no bones broken. When you get in, put a strap round it.'

And then he turned his body from me, and, leaning once more against the boulder, he pulled one knee upwards and rested his hands on the top of it. He looked across the water, and I looked across the water, and there was a profound silence between us. The silence grew until it seemed to my mind to become almost a solid thing. It filled the air and spread over the ground with a stillness that quietened the spirit. It was all around me, in me. The essence of that moment will remain with me until I die. Then I remember the atmosphere in the silence changing; it was as if his presence had impregnated it, now forcing an awareness on me. When I became conscious of him, I experienced another strange feeling. I felt that this man and I – this man whom I disliked for most of the qualities he had shown to me – this man and I shared something. It seemed as if we were thinking along the same channels – but what particular channels, I, as yet, didn't put a name to.

I came to myself as a single blade of glass flickered; the movement stood out against the stillness like a water spout in a calm sea. My head turned downwards so I could look at the fluttering blade. It was at this moment that my companion began to talk.

McVeigh was still looking over the water as he said, 'When I got this – ' he tapped first his shirt front and then his thigh ' – I thought it was the finish; I *hoped* it was the finish. When anything big hits us, that's always the natural reaction – to give way before it.'

He paused, and I asked quietly, 'Was it in the war?'

'Sort of – but nothing romantic.' I saw a twist to his lips. 'No dashing in to save my superior officer. No medals. Just a petrol lorry toppling down a bank and catching fire. They found me with my head stuck out of the window – the door had jammed. My boots saved my feet, but they wouldn't have if I had been there much longer.'

'Where did it happen?'

'In Korea. The big war and all the shouting was over. Things like this don't matter often; and then only to the people to whom they happen.'

'I am truly sorry.'

I was looking down towards the grass as I spoke and I felt his head jerk in my direction.

His voice took on that deep satirical quality that verged on laughter as he replied, 'Now, look here, don't go wasting your sympathy on me. I don't want you or anyone else to be sorry for me.'

His voice, his manner, had sent me back to the steep road and the incident with the cars. Hastily, I got to my feet but, before I was standing straight, he was up, too, and, again, we were looking at each other.

I said, 'I'm not sorry for you. I don't think anybody could be sorry for you.'

My meaning was not what my actual words conveyed literally. I suppose I meant he was too big a man to attract pity; his manner spurned pity; yet this wasn't the reaction my words had on him. To my surprise, I saw a look that was almost pain come into his eyes. His lower lip moved in and out twice and his jaw jerked – it was a spasmodic reaction.

Then, his head bouncing once, McVeigh said, 'That's true, that's true.' There was emphasis as he repeated the words. Then he added, 'Well, I've got to get started. Good-bye.'

'Good-bye.' We turned from each other simultaneously and went our separate ways.

The morning had lost its wonder. Although there was no sign of mist, there was now a chill feeling in the air. I was through the belt of trees and nearing the drystone wall when there came over me an impulse for urgency – I wanted to run. If I had asked, where to? – I would have got the reply, 'Home', and home for me spelt Aunt Maggie. I wanted to be near Aunt Maggie, wrapped round by her commonsense, her matter-of-factness. I wanted to touch on her life, a life that had known no unnatural fear.

Yet if I had probed within further and asked why this pressing need, I would have found it was because, deep within me at this moment, although I would not recognize it, was the knowledge of the utter fallibility of impressions, impressions that people gave you of strength. The impression I had first got of Davie McVeigh had been one of strength, perhaps cruel physical strength, but, nevertheless, strength. Now I knew that in that moment of silence when our thoughts had been channelled together, the cores of our beings had recognized, each in the other, the emotion which had dominated our lives – and the emotion was fear. My fear was, and had always been, fear of people and what they might do to me. What they usually did was cast me off in one way or another. My fear had become contorted of late and had acquired strange tangents, but at its root was the fear of particular people and what they could do to me. But what was McVeigh's fear? I did not know – only that it existed.

When I rounded the foot of the hill and saw Aunt Maggie standing at the door in her dressing-gown I ran towards her – actually like a child running to its mother.

And, like a mother, she greeted me harshly. 'Where on earth have you been at this time of the morning? You had me worried.'

'I couldn't sleep, I went out to see the sunrise. But what's the matter with you?' I was speaking casually now. I was within the ring of security; for the moment, I was without fear. 'You are never up at this time.'

'I've got the toothache.'

'Oh, Aunt Maggie, not again!'

She turned on me now an almost comical look on her face as she chided me, 'You said that to me the other day when I was sick. I didn't want to be sick again, and I don't want the toothache again.'

It seemed a most unsympathetic reaction, but I wanted to laugh. Instead, I said, 'Well, you're having that tooth out, and no more shilly-shallying. You've had it filled until there's no original tooth left.'

Instead of replying, Aunt Maggie probed. 'You look whitish and tired, haven't you slept? Are you cold? You're shivering.'

'Yes, I am a bit cold. I could do with some hot tea.'

'It's all ready.'

A few minutes later, after stirring the wood ash into flame, we sat close to the fire drinking our tea, and apropos of nothing that had been said so far, I made a statement.

'I'm starting a book today,' I said. 'I've got the title. It's *The Iron Façade*.'

CHAPTER SIX

It was strange the effect that my new work had on me. Although, naturally, I camouflaged both the characters and the surroundings of Lowtherbeck, the essence of the atmosphere I felt in this place came through in my writing immediately. But there was one thing which disturbed me; I found that I had put myself into the story. Once again, I was probing inwards. I had been entwined among the characters of my previous three books. My character then had been that of a sensitive, poorly-used individual, but now my character was emerging through these pages as a rather self-centred individual, and I found I didn't like the person I was representing.

I didn't like the character, but I couldn't alter her or remove her from the story, for she seemed an essential part of it. I knew that the action surrounding this particular character would make her forget herself, as I wanted to forget myself, but there was something else I had to bring into her character also. As often, when building a character in a book, it is the character that takes charge of the writer instead of the reverse. I wanted to make this character warm and loving as I knew myself to be deep within. I wanted to make her the kind of person to whom people would naturally turn in times of trouble – a young edition of Aunt Maggie. I wanted to make her someone who could forget herself entirely, even to the extent of giving up her whole life for someone else. This was my early intention, but I could not mould this particular character into the shape I had projected. There was an ingredient missing, and I hoped that, as I went on with the story, it would emerge and I would know how to develop her.

When, in the depth of my bitterness, I had poured myself out to Aunt Maggie, saying I must be a frightful person that all these things should happen to me: my mother and father throwing me off, then my husband turning out to be someone else's husband, and his blaming me for it all. He had said, 'Well, take your mind back. I never asked you to marry me; it was you who did the asking.' It was then that Aunt Maggie had consoled me by saying, 'It's their loss for you're a warm, lovable lass. Those that are deceived by your cool model-like exterior have no depths themselves.' It was a portrait of myself as Aunt Maggie saw me that I wanted to set down, but the portrait wouldn't come alive.

I became so engrossed in my novel that during the next two weeks I saw Davie McVeigh only twice, and then only from a distance. When the weather, which had worsened all of a sudden, became permissible, Aunt Maggie did the daily trek to the house for the milk, and, on returning, she nearly always had some comment to make on Flora Cleverly.

One day, my aunt commented, 'That one's so strung up the spring'll snap one of these days. She cannot stand still a minute. But I must hand it to her, she gets through some work. Do you know she does all their washing? She has about eight lines out in the meadow, full of sheets and things. She must have been up bright and early to get that lot done. And there she was in the kitchen baking when I arrived, and that was half past ten.'

To this particular piece of news, I had replied, 'She's very likely speaking the truth when she says they can't do without her.'

I had told Aunt Maggie about the conversation I had overheard between Flora Cleverly and Davie McVeigh . . .

Then one morning Aunt Maggie came into the room whispering hastily, 'He's brought the wood himself, shall I ask him in for a coffee?'

My first reaction was to say *no, no.* Then I placed the onus on my aunt by asking, 'Would you like to?'

'It doesn't matter to me one way or another.' She was still whispering. Then she added, 'Yes, I think I would, if only to prove I'm not early Victorian!'

She returned to the kitchen laughing. She looked and sounded gay. It was one of her young days.

I was using the refectory table as a desk and I'd hardly risen from it when Davie McVeigh entered the room from the kitchen. I hadn't expected to see him so soon; it was as if he had been standing behind the door. I heard Aunt Maggie's voice and the tail end of her words: 'I'll bring the drink in, in a minute.'

'Am I disturbing you?' McVeigh asked.

'No. Oh, no.' I pushed carelessly at a pile of written work. 'I'm always glad of a break.'

He walked down the centre of the room towards the fire. He did not look at home as he had done on that first evening when he had barged in through the front door, but appeared somewhat ill at ease.

'Are you writing another book?' He was standing on the hearthrug waiting for me to sit down.

'Yes, I'm trying to. It takes some getting into if you've neglected it for a time.'

'That's the same with everything, I think.'

He seated himself now in the high-backed leather chair, and although it was part of the suite, I thought to myself: it's his chair.

He asked abruptly, 'Are you liking it here?'

'Yes. Yes, very much.'

'You're not finding it too lonely?'

'I – we don't mind being alone.'

'Do you mind if I smoke?' He pulled a pipe from his pocket when I answered, 'Of course not.'

When McVeigh had lit the pipe and drawn once or twice on the long stem, he said, 'I was wanting a word with you about Frannie. You'll be wondering why, after I asked you if she could come to the attic, she hasn't been across.'

'Yes, yes. It did make us wonder. I hope she's all right.'

'No, I'm afraid she's not all right. She's hardly been near the house these past weeks. I went across yesterday to see her grannie. The old lady says she's moping. I got her to promise to take her to the doctor's this morning. She's a bitter old stick, is the grannie. I suppose life has made her like that, but it's hard on the child.'

I could find nothing to say to this for Flora Cleverly's suggestion was in my mind again.

Then McVeigh broke the silence by referring to the weather. 'The cold weather has settled in,' he said. 'You won't find it very pleasant in a short while.'

'Oh, I don't mind the cold.'

'I don't think you've experienced our kind of

cold.' He was smiling wrily. 'There's been times, even early in December, when we haven't been able to make a path between the cottage and the house – but you'll be gone by then.'

'Yes, yes. I suppose so.'

I felt my eyes widen in surprise when he rose from the chair abruptly and, walking to the window, looked out towards the lake, and after a moment, said quietly, 'I always meant to apologize for the day of the wedding – not for what happened on the road.' His head turned slightly over his shoulder, but he didn't look back at me. 'That was understandable, at least from a driver's point of view. But I mean the evening when that mad lot came across and Alec Bradley—' He stopped now and, turning and facing me, added, 'The truth of it is, I had a drink like the rest and the effect of liquor on me is to turn me into a creator of rhymes, corny rhymes. When I've had a drink I can set anything to rhyme, but, should I try when I'm in my normal state, I find the process difficult and the result laboured. Yet when under – the influence, my verses are fluent and corny.'

I saw that it had taken a great deal for him to speak as he was doing, so I said lightly, 'Oh, I'd forgotten all about it. But tell me, do you write poetry?'

'Poetry – no, it's just this rhyming. My father had a knack too. He filled books with rhymes, sentimental Ella Wheeler Wilcox stuff; yet to look at him, you would never have believed him capable of even that. He was a hard-living, hard-drinking, tough individual but – ' He looked downwards now and tapped his pipe against the back of his hand ' – endearing for all that.'

'Has he been long dead?'

'He died when I was fourteen; my mother died when I was three.'

And I thought to myself, Flora Cleverly brought you up and you've hated every moment under her dominance.

Aunt Maggie came bustling in now and the visitor moved forward and took the tray from her and laid it on the corner of the table, well away from my writing.

My aunt said to him, 'I've been meaning to ask you, Mr McVeigh, did you carve this table and these?' She pointed to the animals on the long shelf.

'Oh, those!' His voice dismissed them lightly. 'Yes. Yes, I used to try my hand at such things in my youth.'

'They're fine pieces of work. And this table is magnificent. Haven't you kept it up?'

'No, no. There's no time now.' He looked towards the carved horse and the hard lines of his broad face seemed to soften as he said quietly, 'I used to spend day after day chipping away at things like that, wood always appealed to me, but as I said – ' he turned abruptly round ' – there's no time any more.' He smiled and added, 'Thank you,' as he took a cup from Aunt Maggie's hand.

He had just sat down again in the big chair when he exclaimed: 'Oh! I forgot. I've some mail for you.' Reaching into his pocket, he drew out two letters which he handed me.

As I took them, I saw from the postmark and the printed address on one envelope it was from my publisher; the other letter, I knew from the writing, was from Alice. It had been sent to my agent's address for Aunt Maggie had agreed with me, without making the reason obvious, that it would be better if we left no postal address.

As Aunt Maggie was now talking to Davie McVeigh and making, as I thought, a successful attempt to prove she did not talk like an early Victorian, I offhandedly opened the letter from Alice. I say 'offhandedly'; Alice was a link with my painful past and, although I wanted no more pain, I felt an eagerness to learn what she had to say.

The beginning of the letter was to the effect that she had been to the house to see me and found only Mrs Bridie there, in the throes of what she called 'doing down a bit'. Alice went on to say that she didn't even know we had left Eastbourne.

It was at the beginning of the next paragraph that my heart began to beat at a quicker rate, for it began alarmingly:

> What I'm really writing for, Pru, is to warn you. It may not be necessary, but you never know. You see, Ian is out. He got remission on his sentence and he went straight to Mother's, hoping, of course, to find you across the way. Father, I understand, ordered him out.
>
> Then he came to me, feeling sure that I could tell him where you were. He wouldn't believe that I didn't have your address and stated very firmly that he meant to find you. His idea, Pru, is for his wife to divorce him and then to make up with you. He thinks that once he's divorced he can bring this about. I tried to persuade him otherwise, but it was no use.
>
> I think you had better be on your guard, Pru,

wherever you are, because, knowing Ian, I'm sure he'll find ways and means of tracing you. I have no need to emphasize how unscrupulous he can be when he wants anything badly, and of this I'm sure – he wants you very badly at the moment, for, as much as he's capable of loving, he, I think, loves you. But what is vastly more important to him, he needs you if he's going to write, and deep down he knows it.

Two clues he has as to your whereabouts; these are that you are in the North and that you have rented a cottage somewhere. Apparently, he quizzed Mrs Bridie, and if she had known anything more, I'm sure he would have got it out of her. He has the idea that Aunt Maggie will have taken you to her birthplace or somewhere near. He said she has the Northerner's weakness – the homing instinct. But don't let this disturb you unduly, Pru. Yet I felt I ought to warn you.

'Don't let this disturb you unduly.' My heart was racing now. The old fear was filling me again. My limbs were trembling, and I felt sick. I could hear Aunt Maggie talking, but strangely, I couldn't see her, for the room had become blurred, dark. I said something. What it was, I don't know. Then I felt Aunt Maggie's hand gripping my wrist. So hard did she grip that I winced because the sprain in my left wrist was still painful. Her voice was loud around me now, saying, 'Pru! Pru! stop it. Pull yourself together. Come along now, no more of that! – What is it, Pru?'

Nothing that I had been through before had caused

me to faint. I had never fainted in my life. Often I wished I could have, just to blot out all feeling. Now, I felt myself retreating rapidly once more away from all contact with people, and, as I went, I heard a voice shouting, 'I won't see him, I won't! I won't!' And then there was a silence.

I seemed to be dragging myself up through layers of black padding, clawing them aside so that I could breathe. At last I was free and I opened my eyes and looked into the face of Aunt Maggie. She was holding a glass to my lips. When she tipped it upwards a stream of warmth zigzagged down my throat. There was warmth at my side too, and I realized I was lying on the hearthrug near the fire, my head resting against something.

'You're all right. There's nothing to worry about.' Aunt Maggie was speaking softly.

What had I been worrying about? I couldn't recall for a moment until Aunt Maggie's next words brought it racing back into my mind.

'You'll see nobody you don't want to see. Now get that firmly into your head. Nobody can get at you here unless they first get past Mr McVeigh and his house. Isn't that so, Mr McVeigh?'

I started as if I had been poked. I had even forgotten the existence of Davie McVeigh, and, when his hands, which had been on my shoulders all the time, steadied me, I lay still once more realizing that he was kneeling on the rug and my head was pillowed on his thigh.

'As your aunt said, you need see no one you don't want to see. I promise you.'

His voice was low and quiet, it was as if McVeigh was talking to Frannie. I made an effort to rise now but I found I was unable to do so. Then I felt McVeigh withdraw the support of his leg. The next moment his arms were about me, under my shoulders and my knees, and, for a brief moment, he held me against him, as he carried me to the couch.

As he laid me down, I heard Aunt Maggie say hastily, 'I'll get some rugs.'

My eyes felt heavy and I wanted to close them, but I didn't. When I lifted my gaze upwards, his face was not far from mine. His eyes, glinting with dark green-blue light behind the short lashes, were looking deep into mine.

Reaching down, he picked up my hand and held it between his two palms as he said under his breath, 'Don't be afraid, I can't bear to see you afraid – not you.'

As my eyes continued to be held by his, I wanted to ask, 'Why me? Why should I not be afraid?' But I couldn't be bothered. I was tired. Not even the glint in his eyes could hold me any longer. My lids drooped and I shut out his face – and the world. Once again, I was retreating. There was no energy in my body, no purpose in my mind, and I knew that by just allowing myself to drift I could return into complete lethargy – that I would also be hemmed in by the barrier of fear didn't trouble me.

I felt Aunt Maggie's hands tucking the rug around my shoulders, and her voice now had a crisp sound. She was saying, 'You are going to sleep, and, when you wake up, everything will be all right. Do you hear? Pru, do you hear me? Everything will be all right.'

'Yes, Aunt Maggie.'

After a while, I became conscious of soft movements in the room. I was surprised at hearing them, I hadn't gone to sleep. I hadn't retreated. My mind was working again, even calmly. It was, surprisingly, saying to me, 'What can he do? If you were to see him this minute, it would make no difference. He can't force you to live with him. And if we stay here, he'll have to get past Davie McVeigh.'

It was as if Davie McVeigh had heard me thinking, for his voice came to me in a thick whisper from the doorway: 'What is he like, this fellow?'

'Tall, thin—' Aunt Maggie was whispering back. 'About your age, I would say. Very charming manner – as if butter wouldn't melt in his mouth.'

'Yes, that's the sort, the talkers, and they get off with it, don't they?'

'Well, I wouldn't say he got off with it – he was put away for six months. But his sentence must have been reduced.'

There had been no sound for some time, so I thought he had gone, until his whisper came to me again, asking this time: 'Why is it always nice women who are taken in?'

'Search me,' was Aunt Maggie's reply.

When the thought skimmed the haziness of my mind that there wasn't much of the Queen Victoria element about that remark, I realized, with something of surprise, that my attack of nerves had passed. I would not be called upon to spend the next forty-eight hours or even two or three days fighting my trembling limbs and fear-filled mind. Alice's letter had plunged me into the depths, but, like a diver rebounding from the bottom, I had risen to the surface as quickly as I had gone down. This fact left me with a wonderful sense of freedom. I wanted to sit up, even talk . . .

It was well into the afternoon when I awoke. I had slept solidly for four hours.

That evening Janie came to the cottage. She brought with her two extra pints of milk, a dozen eggs, and a jar of cream.

'Oh, this is very kind,' said Aunt Maggie. 'You must thank Miss Cleverly for me.'

'It was Davie who sent them.'

'Oh! Oh, then, you must thank Mr McVeigh.'

Janie turned to me now, where I was sitting near the fire, and asked, 'Are you better?'

'Yes, thank you.'

'Davie says you've got a cold.' She came and stood near me. After scrutinizing me for a moment in her old-fashioned way – I had found Janie to be a very old-fashioned child – she asked, 'It isn't a sniffy one, is it? When I get a cold I run all over.'

When I smiled and said, 'No, it isn't a sniffy one, Janie,' it crossed my mind that it was thoughtful of Davie McVeigh to say I was suffering from a cold.

Janie seated herself on the edge of a chair opposite to me and looked round the room before saying, 'It's always funny to me when other people are living here 'cause I always think of this as Davie's house.'

'He'll have it again shortly – in the winter.'

'Yes – I wasn't being rude.'

'Oh, no, of course not, Janie. I understand what you mean.'

'Doris is coming over tomorrow.'

'Oh, she's back from her honeymoon, then?'

'Yes, they've been back nearly a fortnight. But they live right up yon side of Blanchland, near Hexham, and Jimmy's got a farm – not a big 'un, but he's always busy.'

Aunt Maggie, who was sitting on the couch, asked, 'Were you very fond of your sister?'

'Oh, yes. We got on like a house afire.'

This colloquial saying caused Aunt Maggie to put her head back and laugh. Then she asked, 'And do you like her husband?'

'Oh – Jimmy? He's all right, but he's oldish.'

'Oldish?'

This comment came simultaneously from Aunt Maggie and me for we had both imagined the young bride we had seen on that particular Saturday had been on her way to a young groom. Then I remembered the girl saying, 'Jimmy'll wait; he's been waiting for years.'

Janie was continuing, 'Well, not really old, you know, but a bit older than Davie.'

'Really!' Aunt Maggie's head was nodding questioningly towards Janie.

'Yes, and if she was going to marry anybody around that age she could have had Davie, couldn't she? She liked Davie, but Davie went away; he went to Australia. He was only gone a year, but when he came back Jimmy had stepped in – Aunt Flora was all for Jimmy.'

'Mr McVeigh has been in Australia then?'

'Yes.' Janie nodded her head at Aunt Maggie. 'But he couldn't stick it because he hadn't wanted to go in the first place, I think. Aunt Flora had said she could manage, but she couldn't. It was Talbot who wrote and told Davie about things.'

'Talbot?' Aunt Maggie's head was still nodding. Now she asked quietly, 'You're not very fond of Miss Cleverly are you, my dear?'

'Aunt Maggie!' I cried.

My aunt cut off my low censured exclamation with a quick downward movement of her hand as if she were knocking something away from the vicinity of her knee.

'Well—' Janie was looking straight at Aunt Maggie. Now she asked, 'You wouldn't tell her, would you?'

Janie hadn't asked a question; rather she had made a statement: 'You wouldn't tell her, would you?'

'No,' said Aunt Maggie. 'No, I wouldn't tell her anything – nothing about anything.'

I closed my eyes for a second and apologized to Mr Fowler for Aunt Maggie's mangling of the English language.

'Well, then.' Janie picked up the hem of her dress, and, concentrating her attention upon it, she nipped a loose thread between her thumb and forefinger and gave it a tug. When it snapped, she said, 'I never have been fond of her. She's all for Roy. Nobody else matters. She wants Roy to have the place and not Davie. That's why Davie went away – to give him his chance – Roy, I mean. But it didn't work. She's always putting a spoke in Davie's wheel.'

Janie looked at me now and, with the quick change that is the accepted prerogative of extreme youth, she asked, 'You write stories, don't you?'

'Yes, Janie, I write stories.'

'Davie says you're clever.'

Before I could make any comment on this, Janie went on, 'Wordsworth was born near here, at Cockermouth. He wrote poetry. Do you know Cockermouth?'

'Yes, we went there the other day for a drive.'

'Davie says all the good writers come from Cumberland. Do you know what he says?'

I shook my head.

'If they weren't born here, they come here to die. An' John Peel lived here, in Caldbeck. It's not far.'

'You know your county,' said Aunt Maggie now. Then she added, 'I think you'll write stories yourself when you grow up.'

'If I did, I'd write a story about Aunt Flora.' She gave a little giggle. 'She was crossed in love, Talbot says.'

'Was she indeed? Well, well.'

Aunt Maggie's tone conveyed to Janie that she would like to hear more. I wanted to make a clicking sound of disapproval with my tongue, and I knew that Aunt Maggie was aware of this. Although she did not give me the hand signal again, the movement she made with her body, presumably settling herself in the corner of the couch, told me to be quiet.

'So Talbot says Miss Cleverly was crossed in love, does he? Dear, dear.'

'Yes. She was born here you know, in this cottage.'

Janie jerked her head upwards towards the ceiling. 'And two years after, Davie's father was born at the big house. They played together when they were children. Aunt Flora didn't even like my mother playing with them for she was gone on McVeigh, so Talbot says.'

I did not like the child talking this way and was vexed with Aunt Maggie for pumping her, yet this was a bit of surprising news. I did nothing to silence Janie as she went on:

'Talbot said it was all right when they were bairns, but, after Davie's dad came back from college, he wouldn't look at the side she was on, 'cept to be civil to her. Talbot said Aunt Flora never forgave Davie's father for marrying somebody else, but he would never have married her, Talbot said, in a month of Sundays, 'cause McVeigh was so handsome that all the girls were after him.'

She paused, and Aunt Maggie and she exchanged smiles which showed their confidence in each other.

Aunt Maggie said, 'And so you could write a story about all that. And would you give it a happy ending?'

'For Davie, I would. Not for nobody else – oh, except Frannie. But not for her grannie. I don't like her grannie. On market day she was going to take Frannie to the doctor, but they couldn't find her. And her grannie told Talbot to leave a message at Doctor Beaney's, an' he did an' when the doctor called, Frannie wasn't in. That was after her grannie had locked her upstairs. She had got out of the window and down the drainpipe. It isn't very high – she couldn't have hurt herself very much if she had fallen . . . Do you like Davie?'

I was grateful that this pointed question had not been put to me. Janie, her little plain face thrust forward, was addressing Aunt Maggie in a lower tone.

Aunt Maggie, I was slightly amused to note, was in a bit of a quandary. Her eyes flicked towards me for a second, then, as if coming to a sudden decision, she made a deep obeisance with her head and said, 'Yes, Janie; yes, I do like Davie. Mind you – ' she lifted her finger and wagged it at the child ' – I didn't think I would at first, but I've changed my mind.'

'Nobody does at first, but they all change their minds. Except, that is, Aunt Flora – and perhaps Mr Bradley. Alec Bradley and Davie don't get on. That's because Davie was engaged to Mrs Bradley at one time. It was a long time ago – before he went into the army – but when he came back it was off, so she married Mr Bradley.'

I was relieved that Aunt Maggie had the grace not to press further. We looked at each other and then, hitching herself from the couch, she went towards the dresser and, opening a drawer, she took out a tin.

'Do you like walnut toffee, Janie?' she asked.

'Oh, yes, please.'

Janie's tongue was silent for a time while she chewed on Aunt Maggie's favourite sticky walnut toffee. Then, seeming to remember Davie McVeigh's need for her to do the chores, she bade us farewell, but not before she asked me the embarrassing question of whether I had enjoyed having her, and would I like her to come again? This – from a child whom I had taken to be a shy individual. We live and learn, I thought.

When we were alone, I looked coolly at my aunt and remarked, 'You are an inquisitive old woman.'

Aunt Maggie picked up some knitting from the long wooden shelf, came to the couch and seated herself comfortably before she replied. 'Inquisitive, but not old, Pru – anyway – ' she glanced at me, the twinkle deep in her eye now ' – you got a packet of information there, didn't you now? So our Miss Flora Cleverly aimed at being mistress of Lowtherbeck! Well, well! She aimed high, didn't she? But I wonder why she liked one child and not the other? They both have the same father.'

'If you wait long enough, doubtless you'll find out.' I stressed the *you*.

'Doubtless,' said Aunt Maggie with another deep obeisance of her head.

Then we laughed, after which we became silent . . .

I retired early, and, again, it was something concerning the master of Lowtherbeck that erased the harrying thoughts of my own problems from my mind. As sleep overtook me, I was thinking: And when he came back from the war messed up in that awful state, it was to lose his girl to somebody else. He's had it hard, has Davie McVeigh. I was no longer cynical when thinking of him and less and less did I attach to him his string of Christian names . . .

My attitude towards Davie McVeigh tempered still further as the days went on. In a way, I came to look upon him almost as a sort of protector, a protector against Ian. 'He'd have to get past Mr McVeigh,' Aunt Maggie had said, and now I, too, thought along the same lines. Yet even the barricade he presented couldn't prevent me, at times, from being overpowered by the fear of meeting up with Ian again, for foremost in my mind was the memory of the wild reaction his betrayal had aroused in me.

I had always seen myself as a fundamentally gentle creature, yet there was this mental picture of me flinging myself on Ian and clawing at him with my hands. The violence was absolutely out of character for me – at least, as I saw myself – but it held terrifying possibilities as to what might happen should we meet again. Not that I was afraid now of letting myself go as I had done on that particular day, but the knowledge that the sight of him might arouse that strange aggressive emotion in me again was sufficient to give me frequent, although diminished, bouts of nerves.

So my opinion of Davie McVeigh rose steadily – so much so that, by the Fifth of November, when I recognized that he and I were two of a kind – he ceased to be a barricade between Ian and myself.

The revelation was split, you could say, into two parts: an incident in the morning, followed by another in the afternoon. There were some letters I wanted posted, also an order to be sent in to Talbot, who now obligingly brought in any replenishments we needed on his visits to the farm. It was a very sultry morning, not chilly as you think of November being, but heavy and close. This had been the atmosphere for the past forty-eight hours and I felt that nothing but a storm would lighten it.

I was walking along the hill path that morning, approaching the house by the road down which we had brought the car on that first day we came to Lowtherbeck. As I came up through the kitchen garden out of the shrubbery, I looked towards the house and saw, high up, outlined against the dull sky, the bulky figure of Davie McVeigh. He was doing something to the guttering. Supporting one loose end with one hand, he was hammering in what I took to be a bracket with the other. He was working on the far side of the back of the house where the french windows were, at the corner of the building.

I entered the courtyard from the opposite side, and, when I came to the kitchen door and looked upwards, I could see McVeigh's arm, like a disembodied limb, appearing and disappearing round the edge of the building.

Flora Cleverly was in the kitchen, as was Janie. Janie was sitting at a side table scraping potatoes and she lifted her head quickly and gave me a smile. It had about it a secret quality – we two shared something that Flora Cleverly knew nothing about.

Miss Cleverly greeted me in her usual fashion with, 'Hello. There you are.'

When Flora Cleverly spoke, it did not stop her from working. I had become, over the weeks, fascinated by her seeming tirelessness and her habit of carrying on a conversation while doing two jobs at once. Filling the kettle under the tap with her right hand, she would stack dishes on the draining-board with her left, for example. Had I attempted to do this, something definitely would have been broken.

I answered the housekeeper's greeting, then, looking towards Janie I said, 'You're not at school today. Is Guy Fawkes Day a holiday?'

Janie was about to answer when Flora Cleverly put in, 'No. Janie's had a bit of a cold over the week-end. She says she didn't feel like school. But doubtless she'll feel like the Guy Fawkes party tonight. They can always get better for parties.'

Miss Cleverly jerked her head at me as she went on emptying groceries from a large carton that was standing on the table.

'Do you have a Guy Fawkes party?' I was looking at Janie again.

'Not here,' said Janie. 'Over at the Ponsonbys'.

Mary and Charlie make a big guy and we all take our own crackers. Do you like bonfire parties?' she asked.

'I can't remember ever having been to one, Janie.'

'You haven't missed much.' Again Flora Cleverly was speaking. 'Although—' She paused for just a second as she fingered a coloured box she had lifted out of the stores. Looking down at it she said, 'I used to enjoy them when I was a girl. The bigger the bangs the better I liked them.' She pushed the box across the table now, saying, 'There you are, there's your fireworks.'

'Thanks, Aunt Flora.'

It was at this point that the sound of something falling in the yard, a splintering sound, caused us all to look towards the door and upwards, and brought from Flora Cleverly the remark: 'There's another slate down. He'll have them all off shortly. There'll be no roof left.'

On looking back, I am sure it was when the slate dropped into the yard that this enigmatic woman jumped at an opportunity that she thought too good to miss – an opportunity to expose the weakness of a man she hated and to lessen him in my eyes. But it was much later when I worked this out, and, consequently, realized that Flora Cleverly had the power within her to sense forthcoming reactions. Her hate gave her this power. But her power was not omnipotent. On this occasion, the reaction she had foreseen did not occur.

The housekeeper had her hand on the box of fireworks again and there was another almost imperceptible pause in her talking, then she looked at Janie and said, 'Go and try one in the yard.'

'Now?' Janie dropped a potato back into the water.

'Yes. Why not? It will give Miss Dudley and me a bit of a treat; we won't be at the do tonight. Tucked away in bed, I expect.' She turned on me with her tight smile; then, rummaging in the box she pulled out a large, long fire-cracker.

'Ee! not that one.' Janie recoiled a step. 'That's a banger.'

'Well, can't we hear a banger? There are four of them. Talbot must have put them in for good measure.'

'Ee! but I couldn't let off a banger, Aunt Flora. I could a squib.'

'Don't be silly. You just light it and throw it – well, if you won't give us a show, I'll have to do it meself. Where's the matches?'

Janie's face was now shining with excitement; that is, until she reached the yard. Then I watched her eyes lift, as mine did, towards Davie McVeigh. He had evidently moved the ladder around the corner and was now in full view. He was at the top, his head back on his shoulders and his arms reaching up as he screwed a bolt in on a corner bracket. Perhaps it was the stationary figures below him or the flash of the match through the greyness of the morning that brought his eyes towards us. I saw him staring down at Flora Cleverly. For a short time, he was posed like a gnarled fossilized tree, so still was he. I saw his mouth open and his hand lift as if in protest. Then he was startled into movement, but, even before he started his erratic frantic descent down the ladder, Flora Cleverly had lit the fuse and thrown the fire-cracker.

McVeigh must have been about six rungs from the bottom when the fire-cracker, not a yard from the foot of the ladder, exploded with an ear-cracking bang. At the sound, Davie McVeigh's entire body left the ladder, he seemed to fling himself into the air. When he hit the ground, he did not fall but began to stagger like a drunken man.

I knew I had cried out. I was standing with my fingers covering my face up to my eyes. I was aware in this moment that, had the fire-cracker exploded earlier – say, when he had been near the top of the ladder – the explosion would have automatically caused him to loosen his hold, for, at the sound, he had jumped as if he were leaping clear of something – a mortar shell, for instance.

I wanted to run to him, for he was standing alone – swaying and blinking – but Janie had done that.

Janie had raced to him, crying, 'Davie! Davie! Oh, Davie, it was only a big fire-cracker. Oh, Davie!'

I saw him shake his head once again before thrusting her aside and advancing slowly towards Flora Cleverly like some terrible gigantic creature. She backed towards the granite wall of the house, her tongue still for once.

I heard myself shouting protestingly: 'Mr McVeigh! No! Mr McVeigh. No!'

He was about a yard from Flora when he paused only long enough to grind out – and he literally did grind out the words through his closed teeth: 'You! You devil-ridden hell-cat! You!' His arms shot out and he had her pinned by the throat.

At the contact, Flora seemed to come alive, for she kicked and clawed at him; at the same time, I on one side and Janie on the other pulled at him and yelled as we did so, 'Stop it! Stop it!' Even so, I knew that our efforts were as futile as those of two flies attempting to stop a stampeding elephant. Loosening my hold on McVeigh and gazing frantically around the yard for some means of help, I saw, near a big rain barrel that stood underneath a spout, a large wooden bucket full of water. Aunt Maggie had once thrown a glass of water in my face to shock me out of a tantrum. I now heaved up the wooden bucket, which under ordinary circumstances I could hardly have lifted from the ground, and, stumbling forward, I threw the contents upwards and over him, drenching myself in the process.

I jumped away as the bucket clattered to the ground. At the same time I saw Flora Cleverly collapse against the wall, then slowly slide to the ground.

I watched Davie McVeigh shake himself, then slowly push his sodden hair up out of his eyes and over the top of his head. When he looked at me, it was as if he were coming out of a dream, and as if we were all figments of that dream without a trace of reality. Then he moved like a drunken man, aiming, to steady his gait, directly towards the door of the cave. Behind him, tentatively suiting her steps to keep a short distance between them, went Janie.

It wasn't until the door had closed on them both that I turned my trembling attention to Flora Cleverly. She was on her hands and knees now, making an effort to rise. I helped her to her feet, assisted her into the kitchen, and sat her in a chair.

'Can I get you something? Have – have you any brandy?'

Flora Cleverly moved her fingers round her

throat, then stretched her neck. Her wrinkled skin was the colour of dirty ivory. She swallowed, then pointing to a cupboard high up on the wall of the kitchen to the right, she muttered, 'My pills.'

I had to stand on a stool before I could open the door of the cupboard. Inside there were a number of small medicine bottles, all holding tablets of different sizes and colours. I took three into my hand and brought them to her. She picked a bottle that held round white tablets, and, after I got her a glass of water, she swallowed two of them.

'Will I make you a cup of tea?'

Flora swallowed again, then said, 'It's made – on the hob.'

After she had sipped at the tea in her pseudo-refined fashion, she looked up at me, straight into my eyes, and said, 'He's mad. I could have him locked up, put away. You witnessed this, didn't you?'

I felt myself suddenly recoil from her. I wanted to step back, but was prevented by the force of her stare.

'This isn't the first time it's happened, but this time I've got a witness and there'll be marks to show –' she touched her neck gently '– besides what I did to his face.' Her lips came together in a tight thin bitter line. 'I've warned him – I've got him now. I'll ring Doctor Kemp and let him judge Davie's condition.'

As she stroked her neck again, I moved from her, and, speaking very quietly, I said, 'You must remember that it was you who threw the fire-cracker, Miss Cleverly. If he had been further up the ladder, I am sure he would still have jumped. He – he could have broken his neck. What he did was under great stress – emotional reaction.'

'You're for him, aren't you?' There was something frightening in her voice. 'Fascinated like a snake by the great big tough he-man.'

'Miss Cleverly!' My voice was haughty.

'Oh, Miss Dudley, I've seen this all happen before. You'll get your eyes opened before long.'

'I don't need to have my eyes opened, Miss Cleverly. And whatever discord exists between you and Mr McVeigh has nothing to do with me – I'd like you to understand that. And what is more, we won't be here much longer. Our lease is nearly up. Perhaps it's just as well.'

'Yes. Yes, of course. I'm sorry, Miss Dudley. I'm not meself at the moment – that's understandable.' Flora pulled herself upwards and steadied herself against the table. Then, speaking to me over her shoulder, she said, 'You needn't stay; I'll be all right.'

Without another word, I left the kitchen and, taking the short cut, I went back to the cottage, the order for Talbot still in my pocket, as well as the mail.

When I got in, I said to Aunt Maggie, 'Give me something to drink – a brandy and soda or something.'

'A brandy and soda?' Aunt Maggie looked at me through narrowed lids. 'What's happened?'

'Give me a drink first. Then I'll tell you.'

After I had drunk the brandy and soda at a speed that brandy and soda should never be drunk, I gasped and said, 'Davie McVeigh is terrified of noise, and he nearly throttled Miss Cleverly.'

'Dear God!' said Aunt Maggie. 'What next?'

Then putting out her hand, she said, 'You're wet, lass.'

'Yes, I had to throw a bucket of water over him.'

'You – what?' She had just seated herself, and my statement brought her immediately to her feet. With her hand pressed against her cheek, she repeated, 'You – *what*?'

When the brandy had steadied me, I related in detail what had happened. I finished by saying, 'I think I'll be glad when we're gone.'

'Will you?'

I had expected Aunt Maggie to say with me, 'Me, too.' But now, resuming her seat once again and stretching her hand out to the blaze, she leant towards the fire as she said, 'You know, I'm sort of sorry for that fellow.'

'But he would have choked her to death!'

'A man doesn't do that unless he's been driven to the limit. I never liked that woman from the first time I saw her, and I've liked her less every time I've met her since. And, from what you say, she threw the fire-cracker deliberately.'

'Yes – ' I nodded my head slowly ' – I'm sure she did that.'

'Well, then, she deserved all she got. She must have known what an effect it would have on him. She's a nasty piece of work, I tell you.'

I rose to my feet now and began to walk around the room, and Aunt Maggie, raising her head, glanced towards me, saying, 'Go and change your dress, you don't want to get cold.'

'I'll have to go out,' I said. 'I didn't post the letters or leave the order.'

She looked towards the windows. 'There's going

to be a storm and you don't want to be caught out with the car, do you?' She knew that I didn't like driving in a storm, not even through rain.

'I wasn't thinking of taking the car,' I said. 'We can manage with what we have in the larder, but I must get these letters off. I'll go up to the pillar box at the crossroads.'

In my ramblings, I had found that if, instead of taking the back path to the farmyard, I crossed the field beyond the 'kiosk', as we called our unmodern convenience, climbed one of the innumerable dry-stone walls, and went over yet another field and up a very steep incline, I came out just at the top of the steep track down which I had brought the car on that memorable wedding Saturday. And here, affixed to a telegraph pole, was a letter box; I had used it before on a few occasions.

I said now, 'If I hurry, I'll likely make it before the storm breaks.'

'Go and change your dress first.'

'It isn't very wet,' I said. 'It was just splashed – it's nothing. I won't be long.'

'You'll catch—'

'I won't.'

I lifted a light mack off the hook on the back of the kitchen door as I went out and put it on as I walked hastily to the copse, then through it into the open fields. The air was still, the sky was low, so low that there came to my mind a favourite story from my childhood of Henny Penny and Cocky Locky hurrying to tell the King the sky was going to fall. It seemed incongruous that I should think such childish thoughts at this moment, but, looking upwards, I could imagine that the sky was touching the top of the hill.

Long before I reached the summit, I was breathing heavily. Little rivulets of sweat were running down my face, and, as I walked, I heard the first roll of thunder. It was quite near. I'd heard no distant rumbles leading up to it that would have made me think, in Aunt Maggie's idiom, 'Somebody's getting it.' But, by the time I reached the top and the three roads were in sight, I was telling myself I wouldn't make it back home before the rain came.

I had just put the letters in the box when a flash of lightning, streaking across the open fells towards my right, caused me to screw up my eyes and lower my head. Then, right above me, the heavens seemed to split in two. The crash of thunder brought my shoulders hunching and my back bending as if to ward off some gigantic pressure. I turned about now and ran towards the hill.

I could make home, I guessed, in ten minutes. At that moment, I wasn't taking into account any rain. It came with the suddenness of the lightning itself and, strangely, it did not appear to come straight down but struck at me horizontally from the direction of the fells. One minute everything had been so still; now there was turmoil all about me. I could see scarcely a yard ahead, and even this distance was obliterated when my coat whirled upwards like an inverted umbrella. I dizzied round once or twice, thrusting my clothes down, and I suppose it was this that altered my direction. I was running, not away from the road in the direction of the fields and the cottage, but down by the side of it.

I discovered this when I got myself caught up in some brambles. I have described before how this track was overshadowed by trees and heavy with undergrowth and I was now among the low undergrowth. Recognizing this, it came to me that it was better than being in the open fields and that lower down, almost at the foot of the incline, there was an inlet.

I had investigated this one day after seeing Floss galloping, as it were, straight out of the hillside. I'd heard a whistle; then the dog had come bounding out of a large hole. It was, I remembered, some way down the path in a space clear of undergrowth. That's why it had seemed so strange seeing the dog apparently leaping out of the hillside.

The weight of the rain was almost bearing me down to the ground, and it was more by blind groping than by any knowledge of its position that I came upon the aperture. I stood about a yard inside it, leaning heavily against the wall, gasping and spluttering. When my breathing steadied, I straightened up and leant my head back. My eyes were closed, perhaps that was why when I opened them my sight was more accustomed to the dimness and I saw Davie McVeigh.

He was sitting on the ground not two yards from me with his knees up, his elbows on them, and his hands hanging between them. His broad face was turned towards me and it bore the evidence of Flora Cleverly's handiwork.

The bolt hole!

Flora Cleverly's words seemed to fill the small space: *'You were likely in your bolt hole.'* Was this

his bolt hole? Yes. And he had bolted to it after the incident in the courtyard.

At the sight of him, my heart had given a quick jump, and, when it slowed, I was about to say, 'It's a dreadful storm,' or some such ordinary remark. But, when I looked at Davie, at his face – all eyes – deep and pain-filled with self-condemnation, I could not utter a word.

I still remained pressed against the wall and he remained sitting in the same position with his knees up. There was only the sound of the rain, yet it seemed distant and far away. As during that morning by the Big Water, a silence enveloped us. In that other silence, I had asked a question; and in this silence, I was getting the answer.

This man was fear-ringed. He wasn't, like me, afraid of people – his fear went deeper. His were intangible fears, the kind of fears I only touched on when I became filled with fear of fear. I recalled a woman I had met when I was having psychiatric treatment. This woman was afraid of the moon; she also felt that if she walked one step forward she would topple over the edge of the earth. Hers was an elemental fear, and it was the kind of fear that Davie McVeigh suffered from – part of it was manifested by his fear of noise.

If I wanted proof of my surmise, I received it almost at that instant, for, crashing through the silence, came a terrific burst of thunder. It broke directly overhead and seemed as if it were rending the hill into splinters. One moment I had been looking down into his upturned face, the next I saw his head buried in his arms, and I was crying inside myself, 'Oh, no! no!' It seemed such a humiliating thing for a man, a big man, to be afraid of noise, afraid of bangs, afraid of thunder.

'Don't worry, he won't get past McVeigh.' Aunt Maggie's words came back to me. I remembered that what they had implied had brought me a sense of comfort. Nobody could get past this man if he didn't so wish it – that's what I had thought. That was the impression he gave. As the thunder rolled, his head went deeper down between his knees, and, as I watched it droop, there arose in me a feeling not only of compassion – and this was strong – but of awe and admiration. This man was afraid, innately afraid, yet he showed to the world at large a bold fearless front. Where he thought it was necessary, he struck out and levelled a man to the ground while all the time the mysterious, unfathomable elements of nature were attacking him through his sense of hearing.

I didn't remember moving from the wall, but I had. I was kneeling by his side, and embarrassment overcame me for the merest fraction of a second as I put my arm around his shoulder. His coat was very wet, the result of the wooden bucket of water, and the feeling of proximity was strange, and it must have been so to him, too. My touch must have been like salt in an open wound, for he turned his body half from me. His head was still lowered, and I not only felt, but saw, the shudder that went through him.

As the minutes passed, the thunder gradually rolled away, until silence engulfed us once more. I could not hear even the rain now. I had taken my arm away from him and was sitting on the cold, but dry, earth looking at his bent form when he straightened up. He turned round onto his hips, thrust out his legs and lay back against the wall. I could see his face dimly. He was sweating. He sat looking ahead for quite a while before turning to me. His body was trembling, and, when he spoke, the tremor made his voice shake.

'And – and now you know,' he said.

I shook my head slowly. I found it difficult to answer him. Then I asked, 'What do I know? That you're afraid of noise?'

'Y – yes. I'm a man who's afraid of noise.'

'I'm afraid of many things.'

'It's allowable in a woman.'

I repeated to him what they had said to me when trying to arouse me from my self-pity. 'You're not the only one who suffers like this.'

'I'm – I'm well aware of that.'

'What I meant was – ' I was stumbling now ' – there's nothing to be ashamed of – nothing.'

It was a moment before he answered. 'Yes, I – I know,' he stammered. 'But I'm such a big fellow phys-physically. "Afraid of noise!" people say. "You – you want to sn-snap out of it, man." '

I now hitched myself back and sat against the wall, near him, but not touching. 'When did it happen?' I asked. 'Before you were hurt?' I could not say burnt.

'All in one go. The l-lorry was caught in cross fire.' He was stammering less now. 'In the ordinary way, the noise would have been n-nothing, but I suppose I had two skins l-less by that time and it nearly drove me mad.'

I had closed my eyes. I could see his head hanging through the cab window while mortar shells exploded all about him. Why did people have to suffer such things? There should be a limit to suffering. When his wounds had healed, it should have been the end of it, but, with him, it appeared that he would go down to his grave fearing noise.

I said, 'My fear is of people – not so much what they do to me but what they don't do for me. They don't—' I couldn't say they don't give me 'love', so I substituted 'security'. 'No one has ever given me a feeling of security. People generally think that security means having money and the things that money can buy – it doesn't. You know, there's a certain street in Eastbourne that you'd really call slummy, but it used to attract me like a magnet. The children playing on the pavements always looked happy, and the girls, with their cheap clothes and their make-up, looked as if they had the world at their feet – this was simply because most of them belonged to a family. Naturally, there'd be bad hats among them, and I knew that a lot of them drank and fought and that a couple of the men from that street were petty thieves. I knew all about this, yet there was some tie amongst them that I always envied.'

I was surprised to find myself talking to him so easily. I had felt compelled to talk to him, not only to comfort him, but to soothe myself. Yet 'comfort' is not the right word here. It was as if, at last, I was able to explain to myself the complaint that I had always suffered from: simply, the lack of love from my parents – which meant that they had deprived me of security. Added to that deprivation, was the betrayal of my love by the man I took to be my husband. The thought came to me that, in talking freely, perhaps I was picking up the reins of maturity. My next action seemed to endorse this.

If anyone had told me three months ago that I would voluntarily put my arm about a man's shoulders, then reach out and take his hand, I would not have bothered to contradict them. Deep within, I would have known the impossibility of such an action and also the futility of making anyone understand the abhorrence with which even such thoughts would fill me. Up to the previous day, I could not have seen myself reaching out my hands to draw this man to his feet – yet this was what I was doing now. I had stood up and, bending over, I was holding out my hands to Davie. He did not take them, but looked up at me, and the muscles of his face were twitching spasmodically, as if he were trying to say something and the words would not come.

When he did not raise his hands to mine, I bent further and took them from his knees and said softly, 'Come on. Aunt Maggie will have a drink ready.' I had spoken as if Aunt Maggie belonged to him as well as to me.

When he got to his feet we were still holding hands. I felt no embarrassment in this, it was almost an elating experience. I could feel the tremor from his flesh passing along my arm. We stood thus, joined not only by our hands and eyes but by our weakness – we were one with our mutual knowledge of fear.

Slowly I withdrew my hands from his, and,

turning, went to the opening. The rain had stopped. The threatening sky had lifted, and I could see the smoke from the cottage chimney moving almost vertically over the shrubbery. I turned and looked at him and tried to smile, but I found I couldn't. I couldn't smile into this big broad face, into what was usually a bold face, but was now so drained as to appear almost bloodless. Hesitantly, I moved forward and he with me, and we walked down the sodden hillside, through the equally sodden fields, until we came to the back door of the cottage. And neither of us had spoken a word.

Aunt Maggie was standing waiting, greatly agitated, but she did her utmost to cover her surprise when she saw me emerge from behind the 'kiosk' accompanied by Davie McVeigh.

As soon as I reached her, Aunt Maggie put out her hand and patted my chest, saying: 'You're sodden. Get those things off. Where have you been? I was worried sick with you out in this. Wasn't that thunder terrible?'

Her voice trailed off. She must have sensed, from the drawn look of Davie's face, that something further was amiss for she started to cover up in her quick prattling way. 'I've just made the coffee. I think we all want it laced. You go upstairs and get those things off.' She pushed at me. 'Will you take your coat off, Mr McVeigh? Go in the sitting-room and make yourself comfortable.'

As I stepped from the steep stairs into the bedroom, I heard her voice going on and on, releasing Davie from tension. I had just stripped my wet clothes off when there came to me a gentle whisper from the top of the stairway. I saw Aunt Maggie's head rise above the floor level. She beckoned me and I went towards her.

'What's happened?' she asked, alarmed.

'I'll tell you later,' I whispered back.

'He looks like death.'

'Be nice to him.'

I was surprised that I should have put this request to her and I felt the colour rush to my face.

Aunt Maggie raised her eyebrows quizzically as she whispered, 'I'll do my best.' A few seconds later I heard her talking again.

When I entered the sitting-room, Davie McVeigh was sitting near the fire in his shirtsleeves. He rose hastily to his feet at my approach, and his eyes were still on me when he resumed his seat. I had changed into a lime-green dress with a broad scarlet belt; it was a very effective combination and I knew that this particular dress suited me. But I had not worn it for a long time, not, in face, since before I had become pregnant. Why I had packed it, I don't know, except, perhaps, that it was uncrushable. Certain I was that I didn't pack it with the intention of enhancing my appearance to attract a man.

Aunt Maggie was looking at me, too, and, of a sudden, I had a panicky feeling that she might make some remark about my wearing the dress. And she did, but it was not a disturbing remark.

All my aunt said was: 'That's better. I'm glad to see you are sensible enough to put on something warm. Now, Mr McVeigh – ' she turned to him ' – let me fill that cup again. As the song says, "Another little drop won't do you any harm".'

The remark was trite, yet it brought normality, an ease, that was badly needed at this moment.

A flicker of a smile crossed Davie McVeigh's face as he replied, 'You're very kind; I won't say no.'

I had asked Aunt Maggie to be nice to him and she was certainly doing her utmost. I cannot recall all she said during the half-hour that we sat by the fire, but it was she who did all the talking, seeming satisfied with monosyllabic replies from Davie and me.

Just before our landlord took his leave, when he was putting on his still damp coat, he asked a direct question, or rather made a statement.

He said, 'Your time is nearly up.' He brought his eyes from Aunt Maggie's and looked at me.

Then his gaze returned to Aunt Maggie as she said, 'Yes – yes, time does fly.'

'Will you be sorry to go?'

Aunt Maggie's mouth opened. She wanted, I know, to look at me, but she kept her eyes directly on his as she answered somewhat hesitantly.

'Yes – yes indeed, we will. Oh, yes, we'll be sorry to go. Won't we, dear?' My aunt turned her round bright eyes in my direction. I had asked her to be nice to Davie, and she was certainly being that – she was lying beautifully. When I turned my glance to him, he seemed to be waiting for it. Was I going to lie, too?

I said, 'I'll be very sorry to leave here.' I made a small gesture with my hand. 'I've been happier here than I've been for a long – long while.'

The room became quiet, a log shifted on the fire and fell inwards; as I turned to look at it, I was surprised to realize that I hadn't lied.

'I must go. It's been nice sitting here like this.' He was speaking to Aunt Maggie.

'But you're used to sitting here – in this cottage.'

'Not like this, not with company, just talking. Usually I'm doing accounts and working out ways and means. And often I'm so tired I drop off and wake up with the fire dead, and it's the middle of the night.'

Aunt Maggie, determined to keep the conversation on the mundane level, said, 'Now isn't that like a man!' and laughing, she rose and moved towards the door.

I rose to my feet too but I did not accompany them. I knew I was afraid that, were I alone with him, the conversation would not retain its ordinariness, but would revolve around personalities. I felt I could not bear that at the moment. I wanted to be quiet to think. I wanted to know no more about him – at that time, at any rate.

At the doorway, McVeigh turned and, looking back across the room, said, 'Thanks.'

The single word dissolved the veneer which during the last half hour had covered the two startling incidents of the day; it was for my help – at least in the latter of the two episodes – for which he was thanking me.

I could make no reply. He turned away, said a word of good-bye to Aunt Maggie, and then was gone. When Aunt Maggie resumed her seat, I was still standing supporting myself against the mantelpiece and staring down into the fire.

'Well, now, what's all this about?'

I felt her waiting for my answer, for an explanation, but, when I spoke it was not to enlighten her, but to question her. Turning about, I asked, 'Is it really possible for anyone to be absolutely the opposite inside to what they appear outwardly?'

'Well—' Aunt Maggie took up her knitting and her eyebrows were arched as she stared at me. 'You're the writer, you should know that. But aren't we all like Jekyll and Hyde? We've got to be, because if people knew what went on inside some of us, we wouldn't be able to bear it – we'd die of shame. We've got to put up, and live behind, a barricade. And I should say that's what McVeigh's had to do, he's had to build himself a barricade – if he's the one you mean. Well, now, tell me what happened.'

A barricade. Yes, she was right. 'The Iron Façade' so to speak. The title of my new novel was taking on deeper meaning. I looked at Aunt Maggie. She was knitting steadily, her attitude one of waiting. I found I could not pick words to describe what happened between David McVeigh and me during the storm.

'He doesn't like storms,' I said.

Aunt Maggie's eyes came up slowly to meet mine. 'No?'

My aunt waited, and, when I did not supply any further explanation, I watched her eyes narrow – an indication that her mind was working rapidly. I felt the flush rise over my neck and cover my face.

Aunt Maggie had the uncanny knack of previewing my thoughts. She had always seemed, as it were, to hold a key to my subconscious mind, and the knowledgeable look that I saw in her eyes now made me want to protest, not only sharply, but angrily: 'It's nothing like that. How could it possibly be! Don't be silly. I loathe men, all men, and, if I did soften, I could not see myself softening for anyone like Davie McVeigh. Oh, Aunt Maggie, have sense.'

But I said nothing like this. I simply walked to the table, sat down, and in a preoccupied manner, began a new chapter.

CHAPTER SEVEN

Aunt Maggie and I were having tea when we heard the knock. We'd heard no footsteps approaching along the stone path. We exchanged questioning glances before I rose from my seat by the fire and opened the door.

Before me, stood Frannie. A different Frannie. She was smiling, not broadly, just with the corners of her mouth. When she spoke, I found that the change was in her voice, too – not so much the tone of voice as in the stringing together of her words.

She asked, 'Can I get some books, please?' Frannie's voice and manner, though still childish, were different. Before, she would have said, 'Want some books.'

'Yes, of course. Come in, Frannie. We're just having tea. Would you like a cup?'

'Yes, please.' When she came to a stop inside the doorway – this was the Frannie I had come to know, still gauche, still childish – I took her hand and led her towards the fire.

'Why – hello, Frannie!' Aunt Maggie's welcome was sincere. 'Come and sit down. Aren't you cold?'

'No, no, I was runnin'.'

'We haven't seen you for a long time; where have you been?'

At this question from Aunt Maggie, Frannie, sitting on the edge of a chair now, hung her head.

'Here, drink this tea. Would you like a sandwich first, or a piece of cake?'

For answer, Frannie looked up at me and said softly, 'The doctor said I was a good girl.' Apart from the surprising context of this last sentence, she had again used the word 'the', she had not said 'doctor said', but had prefixed the noun with the article *the*.

'Did he, Frannie? So you have been to the doctor's. Have you had a cold?'

'No, 'cause I was hurt.'

'Have this piece of cake.'

I passed Frannie the plate holding the piece of iced sponge-cake, and I watched her eyes brighten as she began to eat it.

'It's nice cake – Grannie took me in Penrith and we had cakes.'

'Really?'

I shook my head in perplexity as I gazed at the child. There was some burden gone from her, some weight. What was it?

'Grannie bought me taffy.'

—I had it! The child had lost her fear of her grannie. That's what had been lifted from her – fear. And what miracles can happen when fear is lifted from a human soul – even in a retarded person – such as this child? Already, she was different, more normal. What had brought about the new relationship between the child and her grannie? The visit to the doctor? The child had said, 'The doctor said I'm a good girl.' Why had her grannie been so eager to get her to the doctor? Because she was acting more strangely than usual; or because she feared there was something wrong with the girl; or had she feared that Frannie was – pregnant?

Aunt Maggie's thoughts must have been moving along the same track as my own, for, inclining her head towards Frannie, she said, 'All your nasty bruises have gone. How did they happen? Did you fall down, Frannie?'

I knew where Aunt Maggie's probing was leading, and I did nothing to check her, for I, too, was interested in knowing what had caused those bruises. Frannie's head was again drooping, but she shook it negatively.

'Did someone hit you? Was it your grannie?' asked Aunt Maggie.

The girl's head came up and her tone was alive in defence of her grandmother as she said, 'No, no, not Grannie. I hadn't smashed nothin'. Grannie hits me when I smash things. It was Mr—'

The name had almost slipped out and, consequently, the child was startled into tilting her plate so the remainder of the cake dropped onto the mat.

'Ee Ee!'

'Don't worry, Frannie. It's perfectly all right. I'm always dropping cake.' I was picking up the crumbs. 'Don't worry, have a fresh piece.'

I was kneeling now, and I swivelled round to the low table and picked up a fresh piece of cake and put it on her plate, which I placed on her knee. My face was on a level with hers. I smiled at her and she smiled back at me. As she did so, there sprang into my mind a fragment of the conversation I had overheard in the yard between Davie McVeigh and Alec Bradley concerning the cottage where this child and her grandmother lived. I had heard Davie McVeigh ask, 'But why do you want to get them out?' Now it came to me in a flash of revelation why

Alec Bradley wanted to get rid of the old woman and the girl.

Slowly I took the girl's hand into mine, and asked, 'It was Mr Bradley who hurt you, wasn't it?'

Her thin bony fingers tried to jerk themselves free; her eyes stretched wide, her mouth dropped into a wordless gape.

'Don't be afraid. It's all right, my child.' Aunt Maggie was on the other side of her now.

Frannie turned her startled gaze towards her and brought out rapidly, 'Ee! Davie – Davie'll hit him. Ee! No, no!'

'There now. There.' I patted her hand. 'Don't worry about it. Davie won't know.'

Frannie was looking at me again, and she repeated, 'Davie won't know.'

'No, just us – we three. It'll be all right.'

She nodded quickly now. Then, her head drooping, she muttered slowly, 'Mr – Bradley – was – drunk.'

I'll say he was, I was thinking harshly to myself and wishing earnestly that I had Mr Bradley in the room. I would lash him to shreds with my tongue – if nothing else – for, if he had been here at that moment I may not have been accountable for what I would have done. Aunt Maggie had said that the night of the wedding was like a witches' Sabbath, and, from what I could remember of the scene in front of the cottage, Alec Bradley had decidedly led the witches. In his hunt for strange excitement, he evidently had come across this girl, this child-girl whose mind was held in the fortress of childhood, while her body was in the budding cadences of youth.

In Frannie, that night, Alec had seen pleasures to satisfy his stimulated, unbridled passion. I was certain now, with a feeling of surety, that he had tried to seduce this girl. Perhaps she had run out at night and come across the hills to see the dancing and he had stumbled on her.

I surmised that her grannie had found her missing, then later, observing her physical state, feared the worst. Her grannie's suspicions would be emphasized when Frannie was reluctant to be taken to the doctor's. But her reluctance, her refusing to say how she had come about her bruises, I could see now could be attributed to the fact that she did not want Davie McVeigh to know who her assailant had been. Dimly she must have thought that, by keeping the knowledge to herself, she was protecting Davie. I, myself, was very much aware – from what I had witnessed between the two men – that had Davie McVeigh known the truth about the matter, murder would have been done. Whatever Davie McVeigh feared – it wasn't any man. This child, in spite of her backwardness, had deep perception stemming from love.

But why did she love McVeigh?

The question again brought back to my mind Flora Cleverly's question: 'It wouldn't be you who was after the mother, would it?' The recollection I found repugnant. My eyes began to search the girl's face for a resemblance, any resemblance to McVeigh, but I could find none. Yet, that was no proof that she had no blood connection with the man she so blindly and instinctively loved.

*

'Not tell Davie.'

I found myself blinking, Frannie's words had recalled me to the present, and I said hastily, 'No, my dear. No. Don't worry.'

Frannie had spoken again in the clipped way of a child. But now, seemingly reassured, she asked, 'Can I have my books now?'

'Yes, of course, Frannie. You know where to go.'

She got up from her seat, put her plate on the table, then ran down the length of the room, but, before disappearing into the kitchen, she turned her face towards us and said brightly, 'Grannie says I can have my books home.'

We both nodded at her, smiling the while.

'Grannie's had a great change of heart it seems to me.' Aunt Maggie slanted her gaze up towards me.

'It would seem so.'

'What do you make of it?'

'What do you?'

'Well,' said Aunt Maggie, 'I think the grannie thought that the poor child was pregnant. But, by the sound of it, she's found that the child hasn't been touched and her relief is making her more human.'

'I don't think it was Mr Alec Bradley's fault that she isn't in that condition,' I said bitterly. 'And what if he should attempt it again when he returns. He's still on holiday, isn't he? What then? He could get drunk again.' I was looking down at Aunt Maggie.

'We can't tell Davie McVeigh. That's certain.'

'No, we can't.'

'I think somebody should know though. What about the other one, Roy?'

I paused before I answered; then, with a slow

negative shake of my head I said, 'No, no. I don't think he'd be able to keep anything like that to himself.'

'Perhaps you're right. I know!' Aunt Maggie sat upright. 'Talbot. If anybody wanted to ease McVeigh's burden, it would be that long-faced individual. He's the one we should tell. He may be able to convey to Mr Bradley on his return that his escapade, if you can call it such, is known, and that, instead of trying to get rid of the woman and child he'd better leave them alone.'

My lips twisted as I looked at my aunt. 'You could arrange blackmail lessons, couldn't you?'

'If need be, yes.' She jerked her head at me and we exchanged smiles. Then looking towards the upstairs room, where I could hear Frannie moving about, I said, 'You know, that child's changed.'

'That's what I was thinking. She seems brighter, different.'

'It could be that her mind's starting to move.'

'Could be – perhaps she got a fright. Perhaps that night Alec Bradley did something after all. Good came out of evil. Who knows? If a fright stopped her development, another fright could start it again. Or could it? These things are tricky.'

'Yes, they are. But it would be wonderful if it were true. Anyway, I'm sure there's a change in her – I can feel it.'

The change in the child was emphasized still further when, five minutes later, coming into the kitchen carrying four books in her arms, she said, 'I've got my *Bambi* books. When I grow up, I'm going to work on the farm, Davie says.'

We both saw her to the door and she turned before entering the trees and waved to us.

Aunt Maggie repeated, 'When she grows up.' She added, 'I've got a feeling she's starting right now. I may be wrong – only time will tell. In any case, we won't be here to see it.'

Aunt Maggie sighed as she turned back into the room, and, as I closed the door, I thought, no, we won't be here to see it.

The following afternoon we set off in the car from Borne Coote. We had talked quite a lot about how we would approach Talbot with the subject of Frannie and Alec Bradley. We planned, after seeing Talbot, to go on a round tour touching the coastline, first through Penrith and on to Carlisle, thence on to Silloth, making our way down to Maryport, or, possibly, as far as St Bee's Head. It would all depend on the time – and if the weather held up, which it promised to do as it seemed very settled after yesterday's storm.

As we drove along the hill path, Aunt Maggie, looking down into the valley, remarked, 'You know, I'm going to miss all this, and more than a little. People just think of Ullswater and Derwentwater and the Lakes when you speak of Cumberland, but there's so much more – places like this, off the beaten track. Sometimes you could imagine you were back at the beginning of things – no wireless, television, planes, or motors.'

'You be thankful there are motors; you wouldn't be going to the coast now if it wasn't for them.'

'Yes, you're right.' I could see Aunt Maggie nodding agreement in her reflection on the windscreen. She went on, 'But there's one place I do wish we weren't going to, or, at least, that we didn't have to pass – and that's the courtyard. I don't think we've ever once been past there that Cleverly hasn't been at a door, or a window, or some place – watching out. That woman gives the lie to the saying that you can't be in two places at once.'

It was true that we had never once passed the house without glimpsing Flora Cleverly. Perhaps the sound of the car drew her attention, or she just wanted to look at us to see how we were dressed. Whatever her reason, it brought her into evidence when we passed.

But, as I approached the courtyard that morning, I thought: this is one time we're wrong. And I am sure Aunt Maggie was about to make some comment along these lines when, instead, she said under her breath, 'Ah! Ah! Ah! Ah!'

For Flora Cleverly had not only made a quick appearance at the kitchen door, but came running across the courtyard calling to us.

When I pulled the car to a stop, Flora stopped too, but some yards away, and she called, 'Have you a minute?'

'Yes,' I answered, then waited.

'Will you come for a bit?' The housekeeper was backing away as she spoke.

I pulled on the hand brake. Looking at Aunt Maggie, I muttered, 'Are you coming?'

'No, I'll stay here. Go see what she wants.'

When I alighted from the car, Flora Cleverly had almost reached the kitchen door again, and she turned her face towards me, waiting. But she had gone inside before I reached the door and her voice came to me: 'There's someone would like to see you.' I paused on the threshold and my arm went out stiffly towards the stanchion.

'Come in.'

Slowly, I went into the kitchen. My body was rigid, my heart seemed to have stopped beating; there was an icy numbed feeling from my waist upwards. My throat was not only tight, it felt constricted, as if the muscles had solidified. Before I turned my eyes to the right, I knew whom I would see.

He was standing at the far end of the long table. Tall, thin, attractive, the charm still oozing out of him. He looked no different from when I had last seen him. Prison had not left any mark on him. There was a soft, almost tender, light in his eyes. Flora Cleverly's voice had been going on all the while but I didn't comprehend what she was saying until my body, demanding breath, forced my mouth open and my ribs to swell as I gulped at the air.

Then I heard Flora Cleverly saying, 'Rosie Talbot said there had been a man asking for someone of your name. He was staying overnight at The Bull, she said, so I went along and looked him up. I thought you would like—'

Ian stepped towards me, speaking my name, and, at that instant, I let out a high scream. I was back where I had started. My body was trembling, I was hanging onto the table for support, and I was yelling, 'Aunt Maggie! Aunt Maggie!' I was aware of the startled look on Flora Cleverly's face, and I was well aware that I was making a fool of myself. But I could not stop.

If I had truly improved in the past three months, I should have been able to tackle this situation; I should have been able to face this man calmly and to talk to him as one adult to another. But Ian was not an adult – he was an overgrown boy – and, as for myself – would I ever be adult, completely adult?

My mouth was open again ready to shout 'Aunt Maggie!' when I snapped it closed. Regret was already filling me for having acted so childishly.

Ian was talking rapidly now, his cultured tone stabbing each word through me. 'Aunt Maggie or no Aunt Maggie, I'm going to talk to you. I've come a long way. I've been looking for you for weeks. I wouldn't have done that if you had meant nothing, would I? Think – think.'

I was thinking. I was thinking fast. I was addressing the trembling muscles in my body, saying, *'Stop it! stop it! get control of yourself. Show him.'*

I heard a movement behind me in the doorway. Aunt Maggie and someone else – because one set of footsteps moved to the right of me and the other to the left.

Aunt Maggie was now standing by my side. She was staring along the table towards Ian. Her voice sounded very detached as she asked, 'Well? What do you want?'

'I want to talk to my wife.'

The word jolted my body.

Aunt Maggie then said, 'She's not your wife – you know that. Your wife is in Wales looking after your children, I would think – and that is where you should be.'

'I have only one wife – that's Pru, and she knows it.' Ian was staring at me now. 'I'm being divorced, anyway. But divorce or no divorce, I want Pru.'

'Of course you do – and it's quite obvious why.

You'll never earn a living on your own. You've got a damn cheek, you know, to say the least,' said Aunt Maggie.

'How did you get here?' The question came from my left. Davie McVeigh was standing close to me and addressing Ian. I could almost feel the heat from his body.

Ian was looking past me now, and it was some seconds before he answered. 'This lady brought me.' Ian indicated Flora Cleverly with a movement of his long hand.

'You! I told you, didn't I? You mischief-making—'

'It's all right, Mr McVeigh.' My voice sounded flat, even calm. 'It had to happen sometime, I suppose. The sooner the better.'

'I can't see what all the kerfuffle is about if he's your husband?' the housekeeper interpolated.

'He's not my husband, Miss Cleverly.' I had turned my body round and was looking full at this mean-faced woman. 'He already had a wife and two children when he pretended to marry me.'

'Whatever I did, I've paid for. I've spent four months in prison, don't you realize that, Pru?'

Ian's voice had brought me round to face him again. I did realize that he had spent four months in prison, but it evoked no pity in me.

'I don't think that it is too much to ask that I talk to you alone,' he whined.

'There you are wrong – it *is* too much!' Aunt Maggie was speaking again.

Now Ian was looking at her, his pale face showing his dislike of her. 'You mind your own business,' he said to Aunt Maggie. 'You're as much to blame for this as anyone – cuddling and pampering Pru – that's all you've done for years. If you wanted someone to nurse, why didn't you get married yourself years ago?'

I had to put out my hands and hang on to Davie McVeigh to prevent him rounding the table.

'Get out of here!' Davie's voice was menacing.

Ian turned his angered face now towards McVeigh and asked, 'Who are you?'

'I happen to be the master of this house – that's who I am.'

Ian's glance lifted from McVeigh's face to rest on mine; it switched back to McVeigh again. Ian looked at Davie steadily for a moment before bringing his glance finally back to me. He said, with an effort at control, 'I want to talk to you, Pru.'

I could feel both Aunt Maggie and McVeigh about to speak when I put in, 'Very well, you can talk to me. Come outside.'

'Pru!'

'It's all right, Aunt Maggie, it's all right.'

As I spoke to Aunt Maggie, I turned from her, but, in moving, my eyes were caught and held for a fraction by those of Davie McVeigh, which were saying: *'Let me deal with him.'* And some part of me answered, *'If only you would.'*

But there was a voice in my head, a wise voice which had been trained under Aunt Maggie's coaching, and it said: *Stand on your own feet. If you don't do it now, you never will. This is neither McVeigh's business, nor yet Aunt Maggie's. You have got to prove to the man who played husband to you that he matters no more, your ability to convince him will affect your future success or failure. Failure will mean that you give way to your nerves. He will return again and again until he breaks you down. Success will mean that no matter how you feel inside, you will remain outwardly calm, you will convince him that you are calm, that he can no longer affect you.*

I was out in the courtyard; Ian was by my side. He was looking at me. I kept walking until I reached the car; there I stopped and faced him. We were standing quite close now, and the trembling sensation had started low down in the pit of my stomach.

Ian's eyes were searching my face. He did not speak for some minutes; then he said, 'Oh, Pru!'

He had the power to turn my name into a caress. It fell on me like a stroking hand; but the trembling in my stomach increased.

'It's wonderful to see you. I've searched for you for weeks.'

'You've wasted your time.' The tone of my voice gave me courage and I went on. 'Listen to me, Ian. Nothing you can say, nothing you can do – ' I paused here, then repeated ' – nothing – do you hear me? – nothing you can do will ever make me take up a life with you again.'

'I could make you alter your decision – give me a chance, Pru,' Ian insisted.

I now leaned my head slightly forward and to the side as I said quietly, 'I want you to believe this, Ian. I want you to get this into your head – it will save you a lot of trouble in the future. Now, listen. The very thought of you ever again touching me makes me want to retch – can you understand that?'

I felt at this moment that I was being cruel. As I

watched his well-moulded lips compress themselves into a line, I knew a moment of triumph. I had struck home, I had shaken his vanity. I had known for a long while now that the main ingredients that made up this man were charm and vanity. The two essentials for a confidence trickster, and that is what he was – a trickster of women.

His lips curled outwards now as he said, 'Aunt Maggie has done a good job on you; she's toughened you up. She must have worked hard to have achieved so much in so short a time.'

'Aunt Maggie has done no "job" on me, as you call it.'

'Well, if she hasn't, somebody has.' His lip curled further. 'Six months ago you would have been throwing a bout of hysteria, shaking like jelly, or getting fighting mad.'

He was remembering the night when, like a wounded tigress, I had wanted, and tried, to tear him to shreds.

He said now, 'I can't think your steady equilibrium is due to the Cumberland air entirely. It would not have anything to do with the burly landsman back there, would it?' He inclined his head towards the house.

Don't panic, said the voice in my head. *Don't deny it too emphatically. Don't lift your chin or stiffen your back, for he'll see his answer in the signs if you do.*

I said, 'The experiences I had recently will last me for some time. I don't wish to repeat them in any form.'

His lips moved in a twisted smile. 'It was only a

thought. Yet, he's not your type, I could never see you going for brawn without brain.'

At this, I felt within me a quick reaction. I found I was resenting deeply the implication that Davie McVeigh should be classed as a man without brains. Again the voice said, *Steady, steady*.

I spoke now in a tone that surprised even me with its calmness. 'I want to tell you, Ian, that if you try to see me again, or pester me in any way, I will inform my solicitor and instruct him to take the matter to court.'

I saw Ian wince as if he had been flicked by a whip. Whatever his experience in prison had been, he undoubtedly did not want it repeated. His head began to wag now, his shoulders jerked. I knew the signs – this was the nasty side of him.

I forestalled anything he was going to say with: 'Miss Cleverly brought you, perhaps Miss Cleverly will take you back to the village. Good-bye, Ian.'

As I attempted to move away from him he took a step towards me. His face was livid below his dark hair, and he said through clenched teeth, 'You've gone the way of the rest of them. You used to be different; now you're as bitchy as they come.'

I did not answer. I looked at him coldly, then turned about. But as I walked away from him, my legs began to tremble, for I should not have been surprised if his hand had grasped me and he had held me while he poured forth abuse.

I knew Ian was still standing watching me when I reached the kitchen door. I dared not look back, but I almost heaved a sigh of relief when I stepped over the threshold. Aunt Maggie was standing where I had left her; Davie McVeigh was over by the window – he must have been watching us all the while. Although I did not look at Davie I was aware that he had not turned towards me. Flora Cleverly was not to be seen.

I said quietly to Aunt Maggie, 'We'll go now.'

My aunt said nothing, but walked past and preceded me into the courtyard again. When I reached the yard once more, there was no sign of Ian, but I felt he was still about, standing in some corner watching me. I knew as I walked to the car that Davie McVeigh too was watching me.

Seated behind the wheel, I said to Aunt Maggie, 'I can't drive.'

'You drive that car, lass.'

'I daren't, Aunt Maggie. I'm shaking so.'

'There's no sign of it,' she said.

I was about to turn and look at her when I stopped myself and stared ahead through the windscreen. No, there was no sign of it. I might be trembling inside, but I wasn't showing it. I had won. I pushed in the gears, released the brake, and drove the car past the yard and up the steep bank.

When we reached the three roads, I stopped and said to Aunt Maggie, 'I can't go into Borne Coote; I couldn't talk to Talbot now.'

'No, lass, I understand. Let's go straight on to Penrith. We'll see him tomorrow.'

When we reached Penrith, I suggested we should have a drink.

Aunt Maggie agreed. 'And a very good idea an' all. And a bit of lunch with it.'

I did not want to eat, but I forced myself to swallow the food. After the meal was finished, I looked across the table at Aunt Maggie and asked, 'Would you mind if we don't go round the coast?'

'Not a bit.' Then her hand came out and gripped my wrist. 'You did well,' she said softly. 'Splendid. You never need worry again.'

My aunt's kindly tone was almost too much for me; I wanted to drop my head on my arms and cry.

She must have sensed this, for she said, 'Now, now, don't. He's not worth a single thought of yours, never mind your tears. Say to yourself – it's ended finally – for, you know, you were bound to have run across him sometime. I think that's what you've been afraid of, what you've been waiting for – a sort of test.'

She was right as always. I had been waiting for it as a kind of examination, and I had passed my test.

'Let's go home – let's go home,' I said.

'You don't want to look round the town?' she asked.

'No,' I said. 'Some other time. Perhaps tomorrow or the next day – there's nearly a week left.'

'Only four days,' she replied.

'We can do a lot in four days,' I said.

We had reached the top of the gully road and I was braking the car for the descent when Aunt Maggie, pointing towards the road that led from the village, exclaimed, 'Stop a minute. Look along there.'

I stopped and looked in the direction she indicated, and saw, staggering towards us, in the far distance, a figure which I made out to be that of Roy McVeigh.

'He's drunk.'

'He certainly isn't sober,' I commented.

'Good lord!' exclaimed Aunt Maggie. 'He'll be in the ditch in a minute.'

As I backed the car onto the main road again, Aunt Maggie asked, 'What are you doing?'

'Going to pick him up.'

'I wonder if he'll thank you. The other one wouldn't – not if he were in this state.'

No, I guess Davie McVeigh would not have thanked any woman for picking him up if he were drunk, but Roy was not Davie.

When I reached the swaying figure, I stopped the car and, leaning out, called, 'Hello! Mr McVeigh.'

'Ah, hall-o, there.' Roy stumbled towards the window and leant heavily on it. 'Hallo, there.' He was nodding at Aunt Maggie now.

'Would you like a lift?'

'Bet your life – been celeratin'. Been celeratin'.' He chewed on the words; then grinned as he finished. 'Got the sack – oh, high jinks 'n' low jinks!'

I got out, opened the back door, and assisted him onto the seat, where he sprawled back laughing.

I turned the car once again so we were going down the narrow steep bank towards the house. I could only catch snatches now of Roy's drunken mutterings, but he was talking about us leaving.

'Lucky-you,' Roy was saying, 'leavin' this godforsaken hole. Money to spend – travel. That's it, travel. Lucky-you.'

When I drove in, the courtyard was empty, but, as soon as I shut off the engine, I knew that the kitchen was not empty, for issuing from it came loud angry yelling. And when the shouting penetrated to Roy McVeigh's fuddled brain, he started to laugh. Flopping over sideways into the corner of the car, he spluttered, 'Here we go! Here we go! Up the McVeighs!'

When Roy made no effort to get out, I went around and, opening the car door, extended my hand towards him. Still laughing, he grasped it and eased himself to his feet, but he would have fallen if I had not steadied him. I cast a quick glance towards Aunt Maggie. She got out and took hold of his other arm.

She said briskly , 'Steady up. Come on now. Steady up,' and began to guide him towards the kitchen door.

As I approached nearer, I recognized Davie McVeigh's angry voice so I tried to disengage myself from Roy's hand. But he would have none of it, and, almost swaying with him, I approached the kitchen door apprehensively for the second time that day. As the three of us could not all pass through together, Aunt Maggie released her hold on him, and Roy, stumbling inwards, took me with him. Our precipitous entry brought the eyes of not only Flora Cleverly and Davie McVeigh upon us, but also the terrified gaze of Frannie. She'd had her face buried against McVeigh's waist, and she now turned her tear-blurred eyes in our direction and held her choking breath as she looked at us. In the temporary, yet vibrant, silence that filled the room I led Roy to a chair. After he had dropped into it heavily, he still held on to my hand.

'You good for nothing, lazy—!'

'You leave him alone.'

Flora Cleverly was moving down the long table now and Davie McVeigh shouted back at her: 'You keep out of this. Once and for all, I've warned you,

you keep out of this. As for leaving anybody alone, I'm telling you again, you lay a hand on her, just once more, and I'll shoot you up that hill quicker 'n you've gone in your life afore.'

'An' I've told you – ' Flora Cleverly was leaning across the table towards him ' – if you don't want her mistreated, then keep her away from here.'

'She'll be here as long as I want her to be,' Davie stated flatly.

'Oh, will she indeed? We're getting somewhere now.'

They were talking as if they had the room to themselves. 'I've knocked at the truth before, and now the door's opening, is it?' Flora continued. 'She's got a right here, has she? Because you're the one that fathered her, eh? You're the one that Bill Tarrent was looking for! He beat the daylights out of Minnie to get her to give your name.'

'Shut up! Shut that dirty mouth of yours.'

'Shut up, will I? Oh, no! You've brought this into the open, and now I'm going to give it plenty of air.'

'Aunt Flo-ra!' Roy McVeigh's hand was stretching across the table, trying to reach the enraged woman, but she did not see it. Again, he said, 'Flora! Don't – don't.'

But Flora persisted. 'That's why Cissie Bradley gave you the go-by, eh? She likely knew you were carrying on with Minnie Amble – or Minnie Tarrent as she became just in time – before you joined up. Deny it, if you can – she's yours, isn't she?'

The housekeeper was pointing to Frannie's trembling back. The girl still had her arms around Davie McVeigh's waist, and he had one hand on her shoulder, the other on the top of her head. He was glaring at Flora Cleverly with undisguised hate and was about to speak when Roy, dragging himself to his feet, stumbled towards Flora. When Roy reached her, he pulled her roughly round to him saying, 'No, no. You're wrong. Leave Davie alone.'

'You go and sit down.'

Flora pushed at him offhandedly, for her mind was not on Roy at this moment – it was filled with her loathing of McVeigh. But, in the next second, Roy brought her full attention to him – he turned from her and leaned despondently on the table with both hands. He muttered, 'She's mine.'

'Be quiet! Get out. Don't be such a damn fool.' This was McVeigh speaking.

Roy, lifting his head, but still supporting himself with his hands on the table, looked towards the burly figure of his brother and said, in slow, measured words, 'It's – time – Davie. The truth is rottin' in me. It's time it was out.' Now he lifted one hand up, and half turning his body towards Flora Cleverly, he stated, 'I'm Frannie's father. Now you know, Flora.'

Aunt Maggie was standing beside me, close beside me, gripping my arm. Davie McVeigh was still holding Frannie to him. He had his head bowed and his eyes closed. Roy McVeigh was still managing to support himself drunkenly with one arm on the table. He did this for one second longer, then Flora Cleverly was upon him.

Her hands gripping the collar of his coat, she pulled him upwards as if he were a wooden puppet, and staring into his face, she cried, 'It isn't true! Swear to me – it isn't true, Roy!'

The woman was actually shaking him now. It seemed impossible that such a thin frail woman could have the strength to shake this man. Although he wasn't as big as Davie McVeigh, Roy was of no mean stature.

'Tell me she's his! Tell me!' she cried hysterically.

'She's mine, Flora. She's mine.'

'No, no!' She still had hold of him, but was shaking her head like a golliwog, repeating, 'No, no! It's impossible, you were only a bit of a lad.'

'I was six-teen – sixteen, Flora.'

'Sixteen!' She heaved him once more towards her before flinging him against the table. 'Sixteen!' she cried. 'You couldn't – you wouldn't. I tell you, I won't believe it.'

'What's it got to do with you anyway?'

Davie McVeigh pressed Frannie from him, and, pushing her gently behind him, advanced towards the other side of the table.

Again Davie asked, 'What's it to you? After all it's none of your business. Up to these last three years, you've been paid as a servant – a superior servant in this house, but you've forgotten your place because right from the beginning you've been given too much authority. But Frannie does belong here, she belongs to us both. Roy's her father, and I'm her uncle.'

Flora Cleverly had been leaning across the table looking up into McVeigh's face as he spoke, and she repeated 'Uncle?' And again, 'Uncle?'

Then, straightening herself and putting her hand across her mouth as if struck by some fearful thought, she repeated yet again, 'Uncle?' Her eyes moving slowly towards the dresser where Frannie now stood, she gazed at the girl as if in horror before she whispered, 'And I'm her grandmother!' As if shocked by her own words, she jumped back and gripped at the sink before yelling, 'Do you hear? I'm her grandmother!' Then: 'No! No! It's not true, it can't be. I won't be.'

When Flora stopped yelling, a silence descended on the kitchen and all eyes were on her. Roy McVeigh, standing with his back to the table now, seemed almost sober, and he would have retreated from Flora if the table had not been in his way, for now she was advancing towards him.

When she was about a yard from him, she stopped and, looking up into his face, she cried, 'Don't you understand?'

Roy shook his head in bewilderment. Like someone speaking under the influence of a drug, he shook his head and said, 'No, Flora.'

'Not "Flora" – "mother" – I'm your *mother*!'

'Oh – my – God!'

It did not sound like a man speaking; it was more like the whimper of a woman. Strangely, Roy did not deny her accusation, but accepted it with the exclamation: 'Oh, my God!'

'Don't believe her.' McVeigh's voice, crisp and stimulating, brought Roy's dazed countenance round to face him. Again, he said, 'Don't believe her. She wants a hold on you. She's making it up.'

'Making it up, am I? I've made lots of things up in my time, but not this. Your father taught me to make up stories; when we ran wild around these waters, he taught me all I know.'

'You're lying. It was wishful thinking – it's still wishful thinking.'

'You know nothing about it, Davie McVeigh. He would have married me if it hadn't been for your grandfather. I might have been your mother, too.'

'God forbid!'

I watched Flora's teeth set; they scarcely parted as she went on, ' "God forbid!" you say. Well, let me tell you, I'd have made a better mother than the one that bred you, for she hadn't the guts of a louse. When I went down with him – ' she now thumbed in the direction of Roy ' – when I went down with him, I told her it was your father's doings and she believed me. She knew he was on the prowl in other quarters, and she never questioned a word I said. She was pregnant herself at the time and she whisked me off to Spain with her – to the very house on the coast where she had spent her honeymoon. And she stayed there; she wouldn't let him come near her. He had made me suffer, but by God I got my own back on him. There was only three days between her confinement and mine. Her child died a few days later, and her with it. I passed mine over as hers – him there.' Flora pointed again at Roy. 'It was easy. An old midwife and a drunken doctor with not a dozen words of English between them.

'You devil!' Davie exclaimed. 'I could kill you. As for my father – he wouldn't have looked at the side you were on, and you know it.'

'What do you know about it?' She glared at the glowering man opposite her. 'You were a baby then, and he left you with your grannie all your young days.'

'No, I didn't know. But there is someone who did – Talbot. He had your measure from the first. He knew what my father thought – thought about you.

He might have had his women on the side, but he made damned sure that you weren't one of them. He loathed you, woman. He only tolerated you afterwards because you ran the house and – ' he cast his eyes in Roy's direction ' – and saw to him. And it's because of him and what you did for him that I've put up with you all these years – but now, thank God, it's finished.' He pointed. 'Get upstairs, woman, and gather what belongs to you and then leave this house.'

I watched the wrinkles on Flora Cleverly's face move like rippling sand over the bones, and, at that moment, I could have felt sorry for her. That is, until her lip curled back with the action of a snarling cat and she spat at him: 'You're drawing out the last stave that holds this house together. Everything in the past you've touched has gone rotten on you – I've seen to that! And now you'll never pull up. Your land has gone; the house is mortgaged; you've got nothing to raise a penny on. Yes, I'll go, but, unlike you, I'm not without money. An' I'll sit apart and watch you moulder and rot away.'

I saw that Davie McVeigh was trying to control his rage. He was staring, eyes strained wide, towards her when she turned from him and, looking at Roy with a proprietary air, she said, 'Come on.'

Roy was standing away from the table. He shook his head and blinked his eyes; then he turned and looked at the man whom he had always considered his brother. As Davie McVeigh looked back at him, I saw his expression soften. There was a look of sincere pity on his face. It hadn't taken much observation to gather that, in a way, he had despised Roy, but now he was looking at him as if the severance of an apparent blood tie had left him bereft of something. The look on Roy's face was similar.

Roy, although still dazed-looking, appeared to be sober, and, when Flora Cleverly spoke his name, making it a command as she said 'Roy!' he turned his head slowly towards her, and gazing at her a full minute before he spoke, he said quietly, 'I can't come with you.'

'Roy!' The command was high now.

'It's no use.' He dropped his head. 'I tell you, I can't.'

'I am your mother.'

'That's – that's not my fault. I – I haven't been brought up to look upon you as – as my mother.'

'I've always acted to you as a mother.'

'I can't come with you.' His head was sunk on his chest now.

'Where will you go then?' There was scorn in her words. 'You can't stay here. You have no place here.'

'Are you sure of that?' He raised his head slightly.

'Yes. Yes, I'm sure. Why do you think Talbot's brother, Charlie, left me that money, eh? Because he skedaddled off and wouldn't face up to his responsibilities. Charlie Talbot was your father.' She tossed her head in Davie McVeigh's direction as she ended, 'You are no kin to him. As I said, you don't belong here – come on.'

As Roy's head dropped once again, Davie McVeigh's voice came to him across the table. 'You've a home here as long as you want it, Roy. We've been brought up as brothers, and to all intents and purposes that's what we are – differences or no differences.'

In this moment, something within my breast leapt

up and out towards Davie McVeigh. Aunt Maggie must have experienced the same emotion, for the pressure of her hand on my arm tightened until it was painful.

Roy had lifted his head, and the two men stared at each other until their gaze was snapped by Flora Cleverly letting out a sound that rose and ended in a scream. Strangely, she was not screaming at Davie McVeigh, but at Roy.

'You! you fool!' Flora cried. 'Can't you see he's just doing it to get his own back on me? He'll treat you like scum. And what have you here? Nothing. Nothing but work – work and hard tack. And my God, let me tell you, when I'm not here to see to the table, it will be hard tack. Don't be a fool.'

'It's no use, Fl—' Roy hesitated on the name, then said decisively, 'Flora. If I don't stay here, then it'll be somewhere else, but – wherever it is, it – it can't be with you. I'm sorry because I know – ' he turned his eyes away ' – I know you've been good to me, yet – yet, I must say this. I think I'd have been a better man today if – if it hadn't been for you.'

'You – you ungrateful swine!'

'I know. I know.'

'I could kill you. Do you hear? I could kill you. And after all I've gone through – all I've done – and then – and then for you to say that. And, on top of everything, for you to deceive me all these years.' Her voice was rising to a high note again. 'And to think that – that – ' Flora jerked her head in the direction of Frannie, where the girl was standing tightly pressed against the dresser ' – that can claim relationship with me!'

What happened next took only a matter of

seconds, but it jerked us all into horrified action. Flora Cleverly had been standing to the side of the sink. She did not turn her head towards it now, but her hand jerked out, groped at the draining board for a split second, found what it was searching for, a broad-bladed, taper-edged old vegetable knife, and with all her enraged strength behind it, she threw it in the direction of the dresser. I don't know if I screamed or not – I was horror-stricken – but Aunt Maggie did. The knife had been aimed at the petrified Frannie, but it wedged itself in the outstretched upper arm of Davie McVeigh.

As I saw the handle quiver and the blood flowing from his wound, I had a frantic desire to turn and fly out of the room – fly away from all this hatred and rage.

'You're mad, woman! You're insane. Get away! Get away!' Aunt Maggie was crying now. She was standing by McVeigh's side, and I was there also, but I couldn't remember moving towards him.

Davie McVeigh had said nothing; after the shock of the impact, he had not even moved. I saw that his face looked ashen white and his left hand trembled slightly as it went to the handle of the knife. With a sharp tug he drew it out of the flesh and his shirt and arm were reddened immediately by the blood gushing from the wound.

It was Aunt Maggie who took charge now. She sat Davie down; she ripped up towels. She turned to Roy who was again shaking so that you could imagine he had fallen back into his drunken stupor, and she brought him to himself by saying sharply, 'Get on the phone! Get the doctor.'

'It's all right; it's nothing, only a flesh wound.'

Aunt Maggie took no notice of Davie McVeigh, but said again, 'Do as I say, and get the doctor. As for you!' She was winding a towel tightly around the upper part of Davie's arm now, and she turned to address Flora Cleverly – but the far side of the kitchen table was astonishingly empty. The door leading to the hall was open and through it came the sound of an upstairs door crashing closed.

'Have you any spirits in the house?' Aunt Maggie was speaking to McVeigh as she busied herself to staunch the flow of blood.

'In the cabinet in the sitting-room.'

Aunt Maggie was about to ask, 'Will you—?' when I hurried out of the kitchen into the drawing-room, and, after a little searching, found a bottle, one-third full of whisky. But as I carried it back into the kitchen I thought – tea would have been better.

I poured out a good measure of the spirits and handed the drink to McVeigh. When he took it from me, he did not look at me nor speak, but, putting the glass to his lips, he threw off the drink in one swoop, gave a slight shudder, and closed his eyes as he returned the glass to me.

'The doctor says he'll be here in about fifteen minutes.' I was surprised to find Roy at my side. He was looking down at Davie, and he added, 'Oh, man! Oh, I'm sorry.'

'We'd be all much sorrier if the knife had found its mark.'

The two men were again looking at each other, and I shuddered slightly as I realized that Flora Cleverly's aim, but for Davie's outstretched arm, would have caught Frannie full in the neck, for the girl had been too petrified to move. Thinking of her now, I turned towards the dresser. She was still standing there, seemingly unable to drag herself away from its support.

I went to her and, putting my arm about her, said quietly, 'It's all right. No one's going to hurt you. It's all right.'

Frannie gasped and leant against me.

At this point, Davie McVeigh turned his eyes towards us and asked, 'Will you keep her with you – for the time being?'

All I did was to incline my head in agreement. I knew what he meant by 'for the time being'. What Flora Cleverly had been frustrated in accomplishing once, she was quite capable of attempting a second time.

Now, as if oblivious of us all except the man whom he had always looked upon as his brother, Roy pulled a chair close to McVeigh's, and sat down; their knees were almost touching.

Roy said again, 'Oh, I'm sorry, Davie.' Then lowering his head slightly, he asked, 'Did you know all along about – about us?'

'Forget it – it wasn't your fault.'

'But have you known all along?'

'No. No, I knew nothing about it. I always thought that – that we were brothers and – and, to all intents and purposes, we are.'

'Thanks, man.'

There was an embarrassing silence now, broken by Aunt Maggie ripping more cloth for bandaging.

Then Roy said under his breath, 'I've lost me job; I got the sack. But it's likely all to the good. I'll move on and get something. And I'll – I'll support her. She's mine, and I'll support her.'

'It's a bad time for you to be moving on.' McVeigh was watching Aunt Maggie's hands as he spoke. 'This is my right arm; I'm going to be handicapped with the turning for the next few days.'

'Oh, man, I wouldn't walk out on you; I'll stay as long as you want. I only thought – you would want to get rid of me.'

'Frannie needs an anchor. There's the cottage – we'll talk about it later.'

'Aw, thanks, Davie. Thanks, man. I don't know what to say – only thanks.' His head had drooped further.

McVeigh said briskly, 'The best thing you can do is to go and sleep it off.'

'No, Davie, I'm sober. I've never been more sober in me life.' And getting to his feet and looking in our direction, Roy held out his hand, and said, 'Come on, Frannie.'

The girl, moving slowly from me, caught Roy's hand and went with him. Just as they reached the kitchen door, he looked over his shoulder and said, 'I'll take her home and see the grannie. I'll tell her I'm bringing her back here – all right?'

'All right.' McVeigh nodded. 'But be prepared – she won't like it.'

Aunt Maggie said briskly, 'Don't lower that arm, keep it up.' Then she added more softly, 'How are you feeling?'

'All right.'

'Your looks belie you. I wish that doctor would hurry up.'

'He won't thank you for sending for him for this bit of a cut.'

'That remains to be seen.'

McVeigh, turning and looking up at me now, said quietly, with an unsmiling twist to his lips, 'I don't think any more can happen before you leave.'

'I wouldn't be too sure of that.' This came smartly from Aunt Maggie.

McVeigh, turning his head in her direction, said, 'No. No, perhaps I shouldn't.'

There was the sound of a car coming into the courtyard, and the next moment the doctor was in the room. His manner was casual and easygoing.

He began by saying, 'Hello, Davie, what's happened? Had a kick from one of your Shetland ponies?'

McVeigh made no reply. After the doctor had unwound Aunt Maggie's handiwork, he made no comment either except to indicate that Aunt Maggie should open his bag. Then he set to work stitching up the torn flesh.

The procedure was too much for me. The sight of the needle made my stomach heave. I walked to the window and stood looking out.

'There. There now,' the doctor said quietly. 'That's fixed that. Now, perhaps, you'll tell me how you came by it? You know you were lucky, another hair's breadth and it would have been the artery – not saying anything about the main leader.'

'I had a slight accident.'

'That's evident. How did you come by the accident – if it's not asking too much?'

The doctor had gone to the sink now and was washing his hands. When McVeigh did not answer, Aunt Maggie, after taking a deep breath, said, 'It was a knife thrown at him.'

'Yes?' The old man's head came swiftly round to look at her.

'It's got nothing to do with me,' said Aunt Maggie, using the phrase that people adopt when they go all out to make someone else's business their own. 'But, while you're here, I think you should see Miss Cleverly and give her a sedative of some sort.'

'Oh – oh—?' The doctor was shaking his head. 'Flora? Well, well. As to sedatives—' He turned and looked fully at Aunt Maggie. 'She's lived on them for years. Pep pills versus sedatives; this, I suppose, is the result.'

He was walking towards Davie now and asked, 'What are you going to do about it?'

'Nothing.'

'Well it hasn't been unexpected; she's been ready to blow her top for a long time. Eaten up inside for years. Where is she now?'

'Upstairs,' said Aunt Maggie.

'I'd better have a word with her.'

'Leave her alone, Doctor, she's going, and the sooner the better.'

'All the same, I think I'll have a word with her if you don't mind, Davie. I think I'd better put it to her quietly that she'd better not try any more tricks. I can talk to her; I've had to do it before.'

When the doctor had left the kitchen, McVeigh got slowly to his feet and, addressing Aunt Maggie, said, 'Thanks; you've been more than kind.'

'Nonsense!' she said briskly. 'We just happened to be here. Now we'll leave you for a time, but I'll be back shortly.'

I noticed she did not say 'we' would be back.

Before I turned to follow her out of the room, I looked at Davie McVeigh who was standing now, supporting himself against the table.

I asked quietly, 'Will you be all right?'

He nodded towards me. 'I'll be all right,' he said. And then, 'I'll see you presently.' It sounded like a promise.

I went out into the yard and followed Aunt Maggie to the car. As we drove to the cottage, we did not exchange any words, but, as soon as we were indoors, she began to bustle about. As she did so she talked.

'Well, I've witnessed some things in me time,' she said, 'but never any like today's do. Flora Cleverly – Roy's mother! She's a devil of a woman that. And Roy – Frannie's father! I wouldn't have believed that! If it had been McVeigh himself – well, yes, I could have swallowed that. But Roy going after Minnie Amble, and him just a lad, and he couldn't have had anything about him really, no real attraction, not like McVeigh. He's a weakling, Roy is. He doesn't take after her; he must have taken after the father who skedaddled off and took the line of least resistance. When you come to think of it, it's very good of McVeigh to take things the way he did, offering to let him stay on.'

I found to my surprise that I was becoming impatient with Aunt Maggie's incessant chatter. I wanted to be quiet to think. I was also surprised in the way I answered her last remark, for I said, 'Well, it's to Davie's advantage to keep him here now, for as he said he can't do much with one hand, turning that mushroom manure takes all of two hands – he's going to need Roy.'

I was not looking at Aunt Maggie as I spoke, but I felt her stop what she was doing and turn her eyes towards me.

'What's the matter?' she asked. 'Are you feeling upset?'

'No, no. Of course not.' Then sitting down with a plop on the chair to the side of the hearth, I followed this up with, 'Yes. Yes. Of course I'm upset.'

She came and stood near me, saying, 'Naturally, you're bound to be with one thing and another. The quicker we get packed up and away the better you'll like it. It's been a day and a half, and no mistake.'

I had turned my face to the fire with my head resting on my hand. 'She could have killed that child,' I said.

'She could also have killed McVeigh. You heard what the doctor said, although I think that it would take more than a knife wound to finish off Davie McVeigh. Still I'm really very sorry for him. Funny things happen in a crisis like this: I think he's made an ally of Roy; and Talbot will certainly see that he gets all the help necessary. It's indoors they are going to be hard put to it. Janie couldn't cope – not a child of ten. Anyway, she's at school. Flora said they'd have to live on hard tack, and it looks as if they will have to. Still, I suppose they'll get somebody down at Borne Coote to help out. Yet, on the other hand, it isn't everybody who likes cooking and cleaning these days. We are very lucky to have Mrs Bridie, but, of course, she sticks to us because she's a widow and looks upon us as her family.' She sighed and, turning away, said, 'Well, it's their problem. I'm going to make the tea.'

What a day! Everything had happened that could have happened. No, not everything. It was possible that Davie McVeigh could have taken that knife directly in the chest. What if he had? What if he had died? How would I have taken it?

'Don't be silly.'

My admonition had been verbal and, actually, I shook my body as if a hand were on my shoulder trying to force some sense into me. My inner voice commented: *'He's got a two-inch wound in the arm. It's stitched. It's only a matter of days before he'll be using it again. So stop it.'*

It was quite easy to say *'Stop it'*, but not so easy to turn my mind from Davie McVeigh, or to avoid the new knowledge that had sprung at me. As I sat, I kept repeating to myself: *'This is awful – awful. What will I do?'* And I gave myself the answer: *'Pack up and go right now; there's nothing to stop you.'*

But there was – there was Aunt Maggie. I couldn't understand Aunt Maggie's present attitude. I couldn't understand whether she was for or against McVeigh. One minute she was in sympathy with him; the next, she was telling me that the sooner we went the better. If I said to her now, *'Come on, let's get away from this,'* she would more likely than not say, *'What! Don't you think it would look odd under the circumstances? Like rats running away from a sinking ship.'* I could hear her using that exact cliché.

Aunt Maggie came in now carrying the tea-tray, and she said, as if there had been no break in the conversation: 'I hope the next one he gets will do something to the house. It could be made into a lovely place if a little money were spent on it.'

I did not turn my head towards my aunt as I said, 'Well, he's not likely to have any money to spend on the house, is he?'

'Oh, I don't know. He told me once if he makes a go of the mushroom business, it could be quite profitable.'

'Once,' was all I answered.

On this, Aunt Maggie rounded on me sharply, saying, 'Now, don't be another Flora Cleverly for goodness sake! Have a little faith in the man. Give him a chance.'

I turned my head and looked up.

'All right, all right, Aunt Maggie,' I said. 'Don't shout at me.'

I felt near tears, and, as she turned to the tea-tray, she muttered, 'Oh, I'm sorry, lass, I think I'm worked up without knowing. It's been a day and no mistake. Well, come on. Let's have our tea and forget about the whole business.'

We didn't forget about the whole business.

It was just on dark when there came a knock at the door. I rose hastily from the table where I was attempting to write, and when I opened the door, there stood Janie.

'Hello,' she said.

'Hello, Janie,' I answered. 'Come in.'

'No, I can't stop. I've just brought a message from Davie. He says – he says, will you not come over this night?'

I screwed up my face as I repeated, '*Not* come over?' making sure I had heard aright.

'Yes,' she nodded. 'That's what Davie says. Flora – Aunt Flora's leaving in the mornin'.' Janie dropped her head. 'She's got a van coming. She's going to take the little tables out of the drawing-room and lots of other things. She says they're hers.'

Aunt Maggie was now standing at the door. She asked, 'And are they?'

'I don't know, but Davie says she can take what she likes so long as she goes.'

'He's a fool.'

Janie made no comment on this, but said, 'He looks sick. Talbot says he should be in his bed.'

'Talbot has come?' I asked.

'Yes, he's in the yard. And Roy's there an' all.' She smiled now. 'Roy's working hard.'

'I'm glad,' I said. And then I asked, 'Where's Frannie?'

'She's at her grannie's, but she's coming to stay with us. Roy said he'll bring her back tomorrow after – after everything is cleared up. I've got to go; I'm helping. Bye-bye.'

'Good-bye, Janie.'

As we turned back into the room, Aunt Maggie said, 'He's mad for letting her stay the night. She could do anything – burn down the place; even do him in.'

'Oh, Aunt Maggie! Talk about me looking at the black side.'

Aunt Maggie patted my arm and laughed. 'Yes, I know. Still, I'm sorry he said we can't go over. I had my mind made up to slip across and make them a meal.'

'You had?'

She looked me full in the face now and repeated, 'I had.'

It was as I said – I really did not know what was going on in Aunt Maggie's mind from minute to minute. Nor was I more enlightened during that evening. When we parted at bedtime, she kissed me on the cheek but she seemed slightly distant.

I lay in bed and looked over the lake. There was a wild moon riding, but its light was fitful, and, at times, it was obscured by great drifts of white cloud. When this happened, it looked as if I were seeing the lake through misted glass. As I lay there, I wondered whether Roy McVeigh, when he took over the cottage, would sit up here and look out on the moonlight. I doubted it. I could see Davie McVeigh quite clearly doing just that, but not Roy. I could even see Frannie looking out into the moonlight; even though unable to comprehend fully its beauty, she would still not look at it. There swept over me at this moment a feeling of nostalgia. I was going to miss the place, for here I had felt some sense of security. Over the weeks, I had gathered strength from my surroundings, sufficient to convince Ian that never again would I be affected by him – and that was no small accomplishment.

Following close on this feeling of nostalgia and in direct opposition to it, I began to experience a sense of regret – regret that we had ever come here, for this new emotion that I had now to face up to, and tackle, would colour my future. I was sick of struggling, sick of fighting – I had fought 'nerves' and fear. Was I now going to be called upon to fight – I'd had enough of that particular emotion, more than enough. Why had it hit me again? And why, I questioned harshly, had the emotion to be directed towards – Davie McVeigh of all men?

It was a long time later that I felt sleep coming to me. The moon was full on my face and I remembered thinking: they say you'll go mad if you sleep with the moon shining on your face. *They say; what say they? Let them say.* I repeated the quotation to myself.

My lids were drooping when, through the mist, I saw a figure walking from the lake over the lawn towards the cottage. Standing out against the dark bulk of him was the white sling that held his arm immobilized. I saw him stop and look up to my window. I had tried to keep Davie out of my mind. But now I was going to sleep; I was dreaming – I need no longer be on my guard.

In my dream, I knelt up on the bed, thrust open the window, and called to him – he came and held out his arms. There was no evidence of a sling now and, for in dreams the fantastic takes on the form of the natural, I stepped over the sill and jumped down to Davie. But my descent was not rapid; I hovered over him in the air, in the manner of a Michelangelo figure on the ceiling of the Sistine Chapel, until, reaching up, he caught me and pulled me down to him. As we embraced, I laughed and laughed, and then I heard my Aunt Maggie's voice coming from a distance saying, 'Wake up! Wake up, Pru!'

I opened my eyes and there she was, saying, 'Wake up! You're dreaming. Wake up, Pru!'

My mouth still wide in laughter, I stared at her until, remembering the dream and the context of it, to the consternation of both of us, I burst into tears.

Getting into the narrow bed beside me, Aunt Maggie held me tightly, saying, 'There, there!' She did not ask what my dream was about, nor did I tell her; and, so, we went to sleep.

The next morning when we woke in the early dawn, Aunt Maggie almost screamed aloud from the cramp in her arm. I had been lying on her arm most of the night.

It was now about eleven o'clock. I had been for a brisk walk in the direction away from the house. We had had our coffee and I was settled at the table making a vain effort to get on with my story. But, somehow, it had gone dead on me; all my characters seemed to be marking time. I found I could not use the vibrant material of yesterday, not even if I camouflaged it. Something had come unstuck.

I was staring at a half-written page when Aunt Maggie said, 'I think I'll go for a dander. Better take advantage of the sun. I don't suppose it'll last for long.'

When she returned to the room with her coat on and a scarf round her head, I barely stopped myself from saying, *'Don't go near the house.'* It would have been a silly thing to say. I knew Aunt Maggie would not go near the place now until she received word from Davie McVeigh.

'Won't be long.' She nodded at me, smiled, then went out, and I was left alone with my unfinished story.

Now, I asked myself, what did I want to have happen to these two people – these two main characters? Usually, my characters took hold of me and led me along their own paths, but not these two. I had to mould them, and they would do nothing without me. But how was I to mould them from now on – how? I got to my feet and walked towards the fire.

I knew how I would like to deal with the characters, yet I couldn't do it. But why not? Simply because, in touching on these two lives, I was arrested by a kind of shyness. I had not been confronted with these problems when writing my other books, but this book was different. My writing, the critics would say when they read it, had lost its sting. Some would welcome this; some would regret it, no doubt. I sat at the side of the fire and turned my gaze down the long length of the room.

Would Davie come here at times in the winter evenings and keep Roy company? Would he start on his carving again? No. He'd likely be too busy poring over books and accounts, attending to ways and means. I would never look at a mushroom but I would think of him walking the lines in the caves or preparing 'the gold bed' – as he had once laughingly referred to the enormous heap of manure lying under the Dutch barn.

When the clock on the mantelpiece struck twelve, I turned my face to the window. There was no sun now; the sky was heavy again with rain; and I thought: if Aunt Maggie doesn't get back quickly, she's going to get caught in it.

At half past twelve, my aunt still hadn't returned and the rain had started. I went to the door and stood under the porch roof, looking first to the right and then to the left. I didn't know which road she had taken, or by which she would come back. She might have gone round the hill by the Big Water, or through the back way up to the crossroads. She wouldn't, I assured myself again, have gone in the direction of the house. At this thought, my head turned automatically towards the copse. Then I heard the breaking of brushwood underfoot and thought: she *has* been that way, and I added a mental *tut! tut!*

When the figure emerged from the copse, it was not Aunt Maggie but Davie McVeigh. He hesitated a second when he saw me, then came on, and, as he advanced, I tried to recall the dream I'd had the night before. It had been an odd kind of a dream – he'd been in it, and I'd awakened laughing – then I'd cried. But, like all dreams, it had seeped away when exposed to daylight.

'Hello.' Davie was standing, looking down at me.

'Hello. How are you feeling? How is your arm?'

'Oh, all right. Give it another two or three days and it'll be back to normal.'

'Won't you come in?'

I turned and walked into the room, and he followed me and closed the door. I went straight towards the fireplace and stirred up the logs.

I said, 'Aunt Maggie isn't in, she went for a walk. I'm afraid she'll get caught in the rain. I was looking for her.'

When Davie made no comment, I twisted my head round to see him standing a yard or so behind me. Once more I paid attention to the fire, and, as I replaced the poker, I asked, 'Won't you sit down?'

Again there was no response. When I straightened up and turned about, it was to find him standing squarely before me. He was looking into my face and I into his. Why had I ever thought him big, burly, and roughlooking? His eyes were soft; his lips were kind; his hair, at this moment, held an almost irresistible attraction for my hands – like a magnet, it drew them; I wanted to run my fingers through it. I clasped them tightly and became overheated at the thought.

Could this be me? Wasn't once enough? Hadn't I been through all this before—? But no, I hadn't been through this before. Ian's charm had flattered my intellect while he picked my brains. My present feeling did not touch my intellect, but played heavily on my heart.

'We should talk,' Davie said.

What a strange thing to say.

'Should we?' I asked.

What a silly thing to say.

'I'm not much good at charming platitudes.'

'No?'

'No. I'm going to ask you a question; just answer yes or no.'

My eyes were blurry from staring into his face. The pumping of my heart seemed to be forcing that organ up into my windpipe, making breathing difficult. His features were now becoming slightly indistinct as if a thin veil of mist were floating over them. It was like the mist that covered the grass on the morning that I walked to the Big Water.

'Will you have me?'

What had he said? Would I have him? Not, *'I love you, my beautiful'* as Ian had said. *'I want you; I need you; I can't live without you.'* On, on and on. I, I, I. Nothing like that, just – 'Will you have me?' There was a humility about the question that created a sharp pain, like a jab underneath my breast. Where was the big brash individual who had nearly blasted me off the road on that memorable Saturday? There was no trace of him. The man behind the iron façade was a shy, even humble, being, and a man who knew fear. I had knowledge of the fear, but I had not dreamt of the shyness. Nor had I ever imagined him capable of humility – *'Will you have me?'*

I could not get my answer past my throat. I felt myself swaying gently, then, with an inarticulate cry, I was pressed against him. As his good arm went about me, I seemed to sink right into the warm depth of him. For a full minute we stood pressed close, tightly, tightly close, then, slackening his hold slightly, and with a movement of his cheek against my hair, he brought my face round to his. It was a strange moment, that moment before we kissed, and, then, it was not a long kiss, nor passionate – rather it was tender, tender with the promise of an unusual, compelling love that would control our lives. My head dropped back on his arm.

I was gazing up at him when the trembling started in my stomach. But it was not the signal of fear this time, but of laughter, which I tried to check. This was not the moment to laugh. I was back in the dream – in his arms, and laughing. For a moment, I saw perplexity on his face and a look almost of horror, as if I had been playing a game with him. Then the laughter in me changed and I repeated the performance of last night. A second later, I was sobbing helplessly and we were sitting on the couch, my head buried in his shoulder, and Davie was soothing me as he would have comforted Frannie; only he was using different words.

'Oh, my dear. Darling, darling. Don't, don't. It'll be all right. There's nothing to be afraid of, I'll promise you that. You'll never have need to be afraid of me. I cannot believe that you love me. I don't think you do. I don't expect it – not yet. But it will come. I promise you – don't – don't cry any more.'

'Oh, Davie, Davie, it'll be all right, won't it? Things will work out all right, won't they? I'm – I'm frightened.'

Moving his hand out of the sling, Davie lifted my chin and, looking at me, said quietly, 'I can't speak for you, Pru.'

It was the first time he had used my first name.

'I can only answer for myself,' he continued, 'no matter what has gone bad on me before, this is one thing I know that will work out. There are only a few things we're sure of in life. Death is one. With me, there is another – and this feeling I have for you is it. I know, deep in here.'

Davie brought my hand and laid it so I could feel his hard chest – his seared chest. Again we looked deep into each other's eyes. And, again, his lips dropped to mine.

All I could mutter now was, 'Oh, Davie, Davie.'

Making an effort not to start on another bout of weeping, I tried to return to the commonplace by saying, 'I wonder what Aunt Maggie will say? She should be in at any moment.'

Davie was holding me tightly as he said, 'I don't think she will be.'

'What – what do you mean?'

'Just that she won't be in at any moment. She's busy making the dinner. It'll be ready by now, I should say.'

Davie had turned his head to one side but not

before I saw the twinkle in the shaded depth of his eyes.

'Aunt Maggie – making the dinner?'

'Yes.' He was gazing at me again and he began to smile. '*Aunt Maggie* came over about half past eleven. Flora Cleverly and her vanload of what she termed her belongings had just left the yard when your aunt made her appearance. I've an idea she had been watching – and waiting.'

'Aunt Maggie!' My voice was high.

'Yes – Aunt Maggie.' His face was twisted with laughter now. 'She's a remarkable woman – Aunt Maggie. She's already reconstructed the kitchen. She's having a new cooker put in, all the old cupboards pulled down, and units put up. She's got all her own furniture mentally placed in the house, and, you'll be happy to know, we are to have a new water system and bathroom.'

I was holding one hand tightly across my lips. All I could do was to shake my head slowly in wonderment.

'Your – or *our* – Aunt Maggie is, as I've said, a very remarkable woman. She tells me that, if the business of Flora had not arisen yesterday, she still had no intention of leaving here.' He moved his head to indicate the cottage.

'Oh—?' I bowed my head and bit my lip. Then I said slowly, 'Wait till I see her!'

'Then we'd better go now. The dinner will be waiting, and I wouldn't like to hear what she'll say if it's spoiling.'

Davie drew me to my feet, and, as we made for the door, his arm was about me. He said casually,

'And, oh, by the way, we're going to have another addition to the family – a Mrs Bridie who, Aunt Maggie says, works like a Trojan.'

I stopped. 'Oh, Davie!' I shook my head. 'I'm sorry for you.'

With a pull of his arm, I was caught tightly to him again. 'Go on feeling like that. It's not enough that you give me an aunt, a housekeeper, and – ' he paused ' – a wife. Go on feeling sorry for me, and I will spend my days wallowing in it.'

'But you said you didn't want anyone to feel sorry for you.'

'And I don't – not *any*one – only you, Mrs David Bernard Michael McVeigh. You remember when I saw you for the first time?'

I put my head back and laughed, a free young laugh. Did I remember? David Bernard Michael McVeigh? *My* David Bernard Michael McVeigh. I put my hands up and ran my fingers through his hair.

'Oh Davie! Davie!' It was the wrong thing to do with Aunt Maggie waiting . . .

THE END

Coming in May 1991 from Corgi

WINGLESS BIRD
by Catherine Cookson

Even the approach of Christmas, 1913, fails to excite the restless Agnes Conway, the twenty-two-year-old manager of her feckless father's adjoining sweet and tobacconist shops. There are dark secrets in Arthur Conway's past, and these come tragically to light when Agnes's younger sister becomes pregnant by one of the notorious Felton brothers. And Agnes herself has a secret, which she knows she must keep from her father: an attachment to Charles Farrier, son of a local landowner, who outrages his own pious family by proposing marriage . . .

But Charles is not the only man who shapes Agnes's future, for his brother Reginald makes no secret of his admiration for her; although she could not have foreseen how significant a part he was to play in her destiny . . .

0-552-13577-1
$6.99